KARTER & JAMAR 3

A SPECIAL LOVE AFFAIR

TINA B. & ANAK

Karter & Jamar 3

Copyright © 2019 by Tina B. & Anak

Published by Shan Presents
www.shanpresents.com

All rights reserved. No part of this book may be used or reproduced in any form or by any means electronic or mechanical, including photocopying, recording, or by information storage and retrieval system, without the written permission from the publisher and writer, except brief quotes used in reviews.

This is a work of fiction. Any references or similarities to actual events, real people, living or dead, or to the real locals intended to give the novel a sense of reality. Any similarity in other names, characters, places, and incidents are entirely coincidental.

SUBSCRIBE

Text Shan to 22828 to stay up to date with new releases, sneak peeks, contest, and more....

SUBMISSIONS

To submit your manuscript to Shan Presents, please send
the first three chapters and synopsis
to submissions@shanpresents.com

1

JAMAR

THIRTEEN YEARS AGO...

"Go, go, go, go!" I yelled as I hit the dashboard.

"Shut up nigga; we can't go no faster!" Brandon barked.

"Both of y'all shut up and get us away!" Tiera shouted and looked back at the two police cars that was chasing us.

I looked at Brandon and mugged him. My cousin Brandon always got me in trouble. Since age thirteen, he and I have always been combined at the hip, especially since my Aunty Brenda got locked up a few months ago. Right now was one of B bullshit as schemes. Brandon hit a sharp left and hit the dash down the one way. Cars were coming towards us spinning out of control trying to dodge us. Man, this was like a movie.

"Man, I knew I shouldn't have got in the car with yo dumb ass!" I yelled throwing my gun out the window. I was a little nigga thugging like Cane. My momma tried to keep me away from the street life but growing up where I came from, it was instilled in me.

"Look, I'mma pull in the alley. Tiera, you get out and run to aunty crib." Brandon said and Tiera nodded putting her purse *across her body. Once Brandon hit the alley, I handed Tiera the powder, weed, and the money I had on me.*

"Put that shit up for me." I told her.

She nodded and jumped out the car, running through some folks backyards. Brandon pulled off hitting the dash as we heard sirens in the back of us. Once he got to the end of the alley, a dude came running from nowhere, and Brandon swerved hitting the pole trying to avoid the nigga. Once we crashed, it put us in a daze for a second.

"Get out Bran... Get out nigga!" I yelled at him, and we both opened the door and started to run the same way. I kept looking back cause the jakes was on us. The nigga that made us crash started to run with us. So now it was three of us dodging the boys. We ain't even know this little nigga, but we was out of there. Once we got closer to my dukes' house, the police blocked us off...

"This way ..." The dude yelled.

Brandon and I followed him as we ran in between houses. We jumped a fence and ran out of the neighborhood and kept running. We didn't stop until we couldn't hear the sirens or engines no more. As we put distance between ourselves and the police, I slowed down trying to catch my breath.

"Man, my bad about that. I ain't know they were trying to get y'all too!" Dude said and tried to shake up.

"Nah nigga, we would've got away if yo ass wouldn't of made us crash." I yelled getting into the nigga face.

"Boy first off, they had a tracker on the car. Y'all wasn't going nowhere. Second of all, you don't know me at all, so you better get out my face before I fuck yo bitch ass up!" Dude snapped and Brandon started to laugh. I swung and decked his ass in the mouth, and we started to go blow for blow. I was only thirteen, but I was big out here and had hands. Niggas in the hood bet money on me, and I was winning every time.

"Y'all need to chill out!" Brandon said laughing breaking us apart.

"I'm Brandon, my nigga, and this my cousin Jamar." Brandon said.

"Charles." he said and they shook up.

"Yea, I beat yo ass." I said walking away. He huffed and shoulder bumped me.

"Boy okay. Try me again, and I will shoot the shit out yo ass." Charles said and we all started to laugh.

knew niggas that ran these parts. Niggas over here saw us walking they definitely would try us. I wasn't no punk, though, and Brandon either, so if anybody ran up they were gone get dropped.

"Where you from Charles?" Brandon asked.

"I'm from up north." he said and I jerked my head his way.

"What you doing down here with us folks?" I asked and Brandon and I shook up laughing. Up north was considered the niggas with money. We broke out east; north had all the families with money, nice schools, clothes and cars.

"I'm from north but my stomping grounds is everywhere." he said and I nodded.

"Alright. Where you live at?" I asked. Charles ain't look like he was from up north. His clothes were dirty as hell, shoes dirty and holes all in them.

"I live wherever I want to live. Nigga, why you asking so many questions? Why you little niggas stealing smart cars? Y'all ain't know they got trackers in them?" he asked looking at me and Brandon like we were dumb.

"Nah, we didn't; if we did we wouldn't have taken it. Duh nigga." Brandon said, and we walked up to my nigga Tyree house. I knocked but nobody answered the door. We sat on the curb and waited. I guess for the police to clear out.

"You got a phone on you?" I asked Charles and he looked at me mugging me.

"Bitch, does it look like I got a phone?" he asked, and I stood up ready to go toe to toe again.

"What's up fruity ass nigga?" I said squaring up. He ain't back down though. Charles got in his fighting stance and soon as I threw the first hit he decked my ass two times. I tackled him and got on top of him raining blow after blow. I felt some arms pulling me and that's when I felt a hit and it dazed me. I sat on the curb for a second gathering my thoughts.

"Nigga, why you sucker punch me?" I snapped. Brandon and him started to laugh which made me push Brandon. A car pulled up and my mother hopped out.

"What the hell are y'all doing all the way over here?" she yelled grabbing me by my shirt.

"Ma chill." I said as she grabbed Brandon also and we got in the car. She started to drive off and I looked at Charles standing there. He looked like he was sad that we were leaving him.

"Ma, can my friend come over for a little bit?" I asked.

"Who? Him? Why he look homeless? Oh my God, is he homeless?" she shouted. My mother Eva was dramatic as hell for no reason.

"Ma!" Tiera yelled from the passenger seat.

"Yeah, come on. But soon as we get home give that little nigga some clothes so he can get in the shower. Ain't bout to be stinking up my house." she said mumbling the last part. I hopped out of the car and jogged to Charles.

"Aye bro, you trying to come over and play the PS3." I asked. I really ain't play the game because I was always outside hustling for my OGs. I made enough bad decisions today, though. I was going in the crib and sitting my ass down somewhere.

"Hell yeah. Yo moms coo with me coming over?" he asked.

"Yeah, but she said you gotta wash yo ass." I told him and we both laughed.

"Bet then." he said and we got in the car.

"Ma, this Charles. Charles, this my mama Eva." I told him. He spoke and we drove off.

THAT MEMORY REPLAYED in my head over and over as the casket lowered into the ground. My family threw their black roses down and mine was the last to fall. The tears that I held this whole week finally started to fall. My nigga was gone.

"Son." My momma gently placed her hand on my back, and it sent chills down my body. The rain started to come down fast, and the men from the funeral service let up the big black umbrellas. I walked behind my wife as she held an umbrella over herself and our kids. Everybody in the BGF was dressed in all black. We made sure we beefed up security for these last few days. It was a real thug holiday, and I made sure my nigga went out like a true Guerrilla.

We had to have a closed casket because Charles' body was so fucked up. If it wasn't for the finger tattoo we wouldn't have even known it was him. Then of course coroners identified him. They fucked my nigga up. He ain't even deserve that. That one mistake cost them a whole family of extinction. Whoever had parts in this, their whole family was gone be wiped out by the end of the summer, and I can bet that.

"Jamar." Karter called out to me once she put the kids into the truck. Hearing her voice made me cringe. I was definitely feeling some type of way about Karter. I had so much love for her but couldn't help but think it wasn't God's plan for us to be together.

"Wassup Karter." I asked annoyed and not up for her bullshit. I wasn't trying to be cold towards my wife, but I was hurting right now. To think all this could've been avoided if she let me know somebody was threatening her.

"Can we talk please?" she almost begged, and I shook my head.

If it was last year around this time, my wife and I would be inseparable. I adored her since day one and she couldn't do no wrong in my eyes. Right now, I couldn't even look at her face without feeling some regret. I knew it wasn't her fault that all this shit was crumbling around me, but it seems like it. It's been days since we have been in the same room together, and I still wasn't fucking with her. I love my wife dearly, but I can't fuck with her like that. If only she would've just told me what was going on then we could have got to the bottom of things before it got worse. I can't even believe we lost Charles over this bullshit.

"Not right now Karter. I'll catch up with you at Madukes." I told her, and she sighed and got in the car.

She slammed the door and I hit the side signaling for them to get out of here. It was complicated. I wanted my wife and family, but every time I looked into her face I saw Charles. Every time I looked into her face, I saw all the bullshit that we have been going through. All because of me being with her.

I slid into the backseat of the black on black Suburban, and Little sighed then passed me the blunt.

"This ain't supposed to be happening fam." He vented and I sighed.

"Charles' gone, Tiera went into hiding then this shit

with Jania." Little yelled and punched the seat. The same day we got the package with C finger, Jania and Tiera disappeared. With all that's going on and Teira putting the hit out on Jania, I didn't wanna tell my nigga that I felt like Tiera took Jania.

"We went to Jamaica and tore it down. Them niggas ain't even come out of hiding. We done sent dead homies' heads back to they families and that still ain't bring niggas out of hiding!" Little said and I couldn't do nothing but listen. This was the first time ever that I done felt like shit was out of my hands. We been in this drug game for a long time, and at age twenty-eight, shit been rocky. I was too young to be going through so much.

"It's time to get the team together and gone head and go on out here." I told Little and he looked at me.

"I was waiting on you to make a move." he said and started to type away on his phone.

"First, I need to figure out where the hell my wife is at." Little said and looked at me. "And my gut is telling me yo sister got something to do with it." he voiced and I couldn't do shit but sit there and listen. My gut was telling me the same thing and, if she was moving funny, or even worse, fucking with the enemy, shit was gone get hectic for everybody. "Well, you go handle yo wife, and I'mma go handle mine." I told him and he nodded.

I had to have a conversation with my wife. I knew she was taking Charles' death hard. She was the last person to speak to him, and they were really close since they met. So I know, over all, Karter was fucked up behind that also. I needed to see my kids anyways. Ain't really even spent time with them at all.

Ring Ring Ring!

"Hello?" I answered as my momma name flashed across my screen.

"Look, I tried to stay in my lane with y'all and y'all life but we need to talk RIGHT NOW!" she yelled and hung up. I shook my head and set my phone down. This day was getting longer and longer.

2

KARTER

"Mommy, Uncle Charles not coming back?" KJ asked and I sighed. I didn't want to have this conversation with my children, but the way Jamar been moving, it was time to tell them.

"No baby, Uncle Charles is in heaven and isn't coming back. You know how we had to bury Ashley? Uncle Charles had to leave us too." I told them. KJ hugged me.

"Why is daddy being so mean? Is he gone ever come home?" Ashtyn asked, and KJ looked at her.

"Duh stupid, he have to come home." He told her and she pushed him.

"Both y'all be quiet! Daddy is really sad right now. He'll come home soon." I told them. I knew it wasn't looking good for me and Jamar, and I blamed myself. Jamar's life was perfect before me. My life was complicated before Jamar and I got together, and I couldn't fault him for pulling away from me. Everything happened so fast. He blamed me for Charles getting killed and all this extra shit that's been going on. Jamar and I wasn't the same. I don't think we will ever be the same again. I don't even think I wanted us to be back together. I was going through so many emotions, and Jamar had me sick with him being so cold to me.

First, I couldn't eat, sleep, or even think, but that feeling only lasted for a few days. The third day, I wanted to bust windows and bleach clothes. I was angry! He was handling me wrong. We were supposed to be grieving with each other, not hating each other. The fourth day, I cried and accepted it for what it was. I was done waiting, trying, and definitely done crying. He basically started to take some of his clothes, and I was fine with that. He wanted out then he could get that. I was taking it a step further and hit up a lawyer to draw up those papers. I was done trying in this marriage and at this point he could fight for us but I was done fighting. Knowing him and how he has been acting lately he was done also.

"You alright sis?" Kris asked and I smiled.

"I'm fine. Where is Bran; he just couldn't take it?" I asked. Brandon let it be known a few days ago he wasn't attending the funeral. He took it harder than any one of us! He isolated himself and nobody has seen him since.

"He taking it hard sis. When I talked to him earlier, he said he was just about to go to sleep. He couldn't take it." she said. Something told me she was hiding something, but I couldn't dwell on Brandon and how he was feeling. He would be okay just like the rest of us because we had to deal with it so he had to too!

"Well, I hope he coming to Eva house." I asked and she shrugged.

"He said he doesn't really want to be around people so I just will bring him some food back." she told me and I nodded.

"Well, have anyone spoke to Jania?" Kris asked. I shook my head and I felt chills down my body. I just prayed the niggas that did that to Charles hadn't got to Jania and Tiera. Both of them were missing and the guys was so secretive every time I brought it up they dismissed it and shut me out. That's what I wanted to talk to Jamar about earlier, but he shut me down like always. I was sick of it and before the day was over somebody was telling me something about my girl!

Later on that day...

"I'm good momma, I'm not even hungry." I told my momma, Janet, and she passed me a plate anyways.

"You looking a little skinny over there. You need to eat." She joked, and I sat the plate down and went to go find Jamar. When I walked to the backyard, all talking ceased and I sighed.

"Jamar, I need to talk to you." I stated, and he looked at me then finished typing away on his phone.

"Nah, you gone have to wait, Karter. I was... I was just going to go holla at my dukes right quick." he said and I laughed.

"We need to talk and NOW!" I stated firmly and walked away.

I could feel him following me, and I rolled my eyes. I don't even know how me and Jamar even got to this, but right now I hated it. I hated him even more for pushing me away and putting us in this space. Jamar have always been my protector, and my heart in human form. He has always been by my side, and I was grateful to have him as my husband, but this past six months, shit been going downhill, and at this point it wasn't no saving our marriage.

"What's up?" he asked once I closed the bedroom door behind him.

"Shit, I don't know. What is up? I haven't heard from you!" I told him folding my arms in front of me.

"Is that what you called me in this bathroom for?" he asked clearly irritated. I laughed to keep myself from getting mad.

"No, actually I called you in to see what's going on with finding Jania. Did Little figure out where she was? I mean Her and Tier.." I started to say but was rudely cut off by him.

"Look, we got this shit under control, aight? Jania will be back here soon. Tiera, I don't know where she's at." he said and pulled his ringing phone out of his pocket.

"We done?" I nodded, and he turned and walked out of the bathroom. I shook my head and went downstairs.

"Hey ma. Jamar is taking the kids with him. I'll be back later to help clean up." I told Eva and kissed her on the cheek. I grabbed my purse and jacket off the rack and left.

"Hey, how you doing? My name is Karter Tay... Jackson. I'm here to see a Chandler James." I said reading the name Kris had texted me. The lady picked up the phone and dialed a number.

"Hello Mr. James, Karter Jackson is here to see you... Alright?" she said and hung up.

"First door on your right." she told me smiling, and I walked that way. Entering the office, Chandler stood up and came around his desk.

"Hello, Ms. Karter; it is nice to finally meet you and put a face with a name." He said holding his hand out.

"Nice to meet you also." I spoke and took a seat.

"What can I do for you today?" he asked, and I crossed my legs.

"I heard you're the best at what you do, and I want to file for divorce. Oh, and with full custody of the kids." I told him. If it was fuck me, then it was fuck you too, Jamar!

3

JANIA

"Fuck! Fuck! Shit Tiera." I said and shook Tiera body but her eyes were wide open, mouth ajar and no life left in her body.

"Fuck!" I hissed again and punched the ground. She had one single shot and a little bit of blood on her shirt. I paced the floor and thought about my kids man. I just knew I was going under the jail. I decided to call Little but quickly hung up. He would kill my ass without a doubt; I done murked his baby mama and they baby.

"Oh shit, the baby." I said and quickly turned her on her back. I lifted up her shirt and was so fucking shocked. This weird ass bitch had a fucking fake stomach on like a real deal fake stomach.

"What the fuck?!" I said and sat on the floor. I had to get rid of the body and fast! Only one person I could call, so I dialed the number and waited until they picked up.

"Hello." he answered.

"Hello, it's me." I said quietly. I knew nobody was in the room, but I still didn't want nobody to hear what I had to say. My heart was beating faster and faster by the second, and my hands were sweating so bad I kept wiping them on my pants.

"What the fuck you doing calling me? Bitch, I'm still in fucking hiding from yo bitch ass nigga!" Jason roared, and I sighed. Sad but true, Jason was the only person I had outside of BGF. I know Little was still on his ass for the shit he did to me but I was desperate!

"Jason, I'm sorry but I need your help! I will give you five thousand dollars and help you get out of state!" I rattled off all in one breath.

"Shoot me yo address but I swear to God if this a set up I'm killing you and that nigga!" he roared and goosebumps filled my body.

"Please... Jason, just help me this once." I damn near begged and he agreed. I sent him my location and he was on his way. I paced back and forth and couldn't figure out what to do.

Knock knock knock!

I jumped because I knew it wasn't Jason that damn fast. I looked out the peephole and it was Little.

"Fuck," I whispered.

"I hear you, shorty, just open up." he said and I opened the door. Little walked in and his eyes instantly went to the blood that was on me.

"What the... what happened to.." he looked at Tiera and put his hand to his mouth. "Fuck shorty!" he yelled at me and walked towards Tiera's body. I guess he realized she was dead because he turned back to me.

"Go wash up. Good!" he said and turned the other way to go in the front room. I did exactly that. When I got out of the shower, Teira was getting taken out, and Jason. FUCK, when did this nigga get here. Little looked at me and shook his head; he gave me some clothes.

"Look, I just want you to get away and enjoy some time alone. Don't answer nobody phone calls, matter of fact where yo phone?" he asked, and I handed him my phone.

"Tank and Moe will take you to get a phone before y'all get on the plane. I will call you in a few days when you can come back." Little told me, and I nodded with tears running down my face.

"I'm sorry. I didn't mean for it to ha.." I started to explain but he shook his head. "It's okay, Ma. You had to do what you had to do. I just gotta figure out how I'mma tell Jamar and the family but it'll be okay. I promise I got you, now enjoy this little getaway." He spoke and kissed my lips then hugged me tightly.

Fucking around with this delusional ass bitch I just ruined my whole life." I thought as I got in the car with Little body guards. Fuck.

THAT WAS a few days ago when that happened, and I was going crazy in this hotel. Little hasn't answered my phone calls either. I don't know why I thought he wouldn't feel any type of way. She was his first love, and first person to carry his child at that. The tears slowly started to fall, and I couldn't take it anymore. I dialed Karter's number and when she answered I couldn't say anything.

"Hello... look I don't have time to play these motherfucking games! I just had to bury one of my close friends and just filed for a divorce all in the same fucking day! Quit fucking playing these little games with me!" she yelled and hung up. I sighed and started to cry even more. I was going through it right now and needed somebody here badly. On top of me killing Tiera, Charles got kidnapped. No one probably even knew I was gone, because they were too busy trying to figure out what's going on with C.

Ring Ring Ring!

Little name flashed across my screen, and I quickly

answered before he hung up; then I wouldn't hear from him for another week.

"Little I'm here." I said and he sighed.

"How have you been?" his voice boomed through the speakers, and the tears started coming again. This little baby had me extremely emotional.

"I'm so sorry Little. I'm so sorry." I cried as he listened from the other end.

"Jania." he sighed.

"It's been a crazy week, and I haven't been ignoring you. They finally brought his body to us and as hard as it is for me to say this, it's not safe for you alone. We just had to bury my brother man." he said over the phone and my heart shattered hearing the hurt in his voice. I wanted so badly to hug and be there for him.

"Please..." I started to say but he cut me off.

"Charles funeral was today and everybody taking it hard right now. Bran didn't even come and won't talk to nobody. Jamar got shit going on with Karter so his mind space all over the place, and I didn't even tell him about the Tiera shit because it's just so much going on shorty." he told me and I sighed. I was just praying he told me he was coming to get me. I was pregnant and alone and needed him badly.

"How's my kids?" I asked concerned.

"They're good ma, asking for you. This whole time you been gone Ty'aira asked for you and not her momma." he told me and that made me feel a little better on the inside. I'm not gonna lie. I didn't feel bad at all for killing Tiera. I just feel some type of way that I got caught. Fuck that bitch and if I didn't kill her she would've for sure killed me.

"I'm sending somebody to come get you. I need you so bad right now," he told me.

"I need you too baby." I cried. I'm an emotional wreck

right now; hormones were going crazy day by day. I was going through it.

"Be downstairs in about an hour and thirty minutes." he said and we disconnected the call so I could get ready.

Even though Las Vegas was a vacation spot, I couldn't enjoy it at all. When I got to the entrance of the hotel, it was people walking everywhere. Never mind it was two o'clock in the morning. A black Escalade pulled up, and I hesitated to walk towards it. The driver lowered the window and stuck his head out.

"Little sent me." he spoke and I nodded.

He hopped out and put my stuff in the trunk of the truck. When I slid in the backseat, it was a man in the passenger and another one behind the passenger.

"Put your seatbelt on." the driver said and drove off.

"I'm taking you straight to the airport." he spoke and the passenger laughed. I texted Little and told him I was on the way to the airport. He FaceTimed me.

"Hey babe, I just got into the car." I told him and he smiled.

"Damn, Marcel there already? He just texted me and told me they just landed not even ten minutes ago." he spoke and then looked at something in his background.

"Marcel... Baby, Marcel didn't come..." the dude sitting next to me grabbed my phone and started to punch me in the face.

"Jania! Jania! Baby!" I heard Little screaming.

"Help." I tried to yell but everything went black from the punch he threw my way making my head hit the window.

When I woke up, I was chained to a pole. Around me was dark but I heard steps above me then a door open and shut. After a second, the lights cut on and my head instantly started pounding. I touched my lips and they were swollen, I could only see out of one eye but my vision was blurry.

"Jania, Jania, Jania." the woman said and kicked me in the stomach. I screamed out in pain and my free hand went straight to my stomach. I prayed hard God someway kept my baby safe.

"Please!" I tried to say.

"Please? Please.. please what!?" she mocked me and hit me in the face. I felt blood starting to ooze out my nose.

"I told Jamar I would take a family member every week until he is alone. I meant that." she spoke and kicked me right in the face making me fall backwards. I turned to my right and saw a body crawling right to me right before I passed back out.

4

MACE

"Shitttt. Suck that motherfucka," I hissed as Bria took my whole nine inches in her mouth.

"Shit. Slow down." I said grabbing her head pumping in and out. She reached under herself and started rubbing on her clit in a circular motion, which made me pump harder. I slid out her mouth and stood up while pulling my shirt from over my head and stepped out my pants and boxers. We had just walked into the house from meeting with her father and right now we both needed a nut. The kids were at Mason's crib so we had all night.

"Turn around." I slapped her on her ass as she arched her back. My wife was beautiful as hell and all that meat on her body was perfect for me. I slid my tongue from the crack of her ass all the way to the base of her kitty slurping on her love box.

"Ohh fuck bae." Bria called out and started to throw it back against my face.

I slipped two fingers into her box while she threw it back. "Fuck Mace, Fuck me." she moaned out as she came all on my fingers. Putting my two fingers to her mouth, she licked all her juices off as I slipped my dick in her hole.

"Shit, fuck." I called out as I slapped her on her ass leaving my hand print. I took my time pumping in and out of her cause I didn't wanna nut so fast. I couldn't help myself. My wife had the best sex ever. I have had my share of women in my life but she was by far the best.

I did a few pumps and swirl, and I was burying all my seeds deep in her guts. Every chance I got I was dropping babies off in her. I laid on the side of her sweating and trying to catch my breath. Bria tried to get out of bed but I caught her, pulling her to me.

"Come on, now, bae. I gotta get a washcloth to wipe us off." she said and I laughed.

"Forget that; lay with me. It's not every day that we get to lay up naked with no interruptions." I told her, and she snuggled against me. Sweaty and all.

"I love you, Mace, you know that right?" she asked.

"Of course. You know I love you too." I told her. Every time after sex she always wanted to confess her love to me. I didn't mind though.

"Of course. I think it's time for our families to meet." She told me, and I looked at her. It was her idea to not bring the families around each other. With my work and her family name and where she stands in her family business, keeping her family and my family away from each other was best. I couldn't help who I love so if my family accepted me, they gone have to accept hers and that's vice versa.

"What about…" I started to say and she sat up.

"My father just gone have to deal with it. I'm pretty sure if I tell my pops what's going on he won't hesitate to step in and help y'all with the situation." she told me and I shook my head.

. . .

"I'm pretty sure Jock got everything under control and, as far as them shooting at Kris and fucking with Karter, well they saw me personally." I told her and she smiled.

"So you been handling business without me I see." she said tossing her hair over her shoulder.

"It was personal bae and besides you was at home with the kids. Couldn't pull you from what's important." I told her and she nodded.

"I understand." She replied. We laid there for about thirty minutes and both our alarms started going off. She got up first and headed to the shower. I heard the water running so I decided to join her. The water touched my skin, and I fell, tripping over my own feet trying not to let the water touch me anymore.

"Damn man, turn that fucking cold water on!" I hissed, rubbing the side of my leg that I fell on. It was fucking with me, and I know by the morning my shit was gone be swole.

"My shit gone be fucked up in the morning." I whined limping back into the shower.

After we showered for about twenty minutes, we both stepped out. I was slower than her because my leg was still hurting. Brea helped me dry off as I slid on some boxers and black sweatpants. I threw my black shirt over my head and my black hoodie on afterwards then slipped on some black Timberlands. After getting fully dressed, I looked up to Brea standing in the doorway fully dressed in all black with a duffle bag in her hand.

"Ready grandpa?" she asked and laughed.

"Fuck You!" I hissed and grabbed my gloves.

Pulling on the block, Brea pulled a little ways down from the address on the paper and cut the lights and car off. I gave her the gun, and we both exited the car. When we got to the building, nobody was out there. Bria grabbed the knife and jammed it in the lock and it popped open. I smiled proudly because I taught her everything she knows. We took the emergency stairs all the way to the fifth floor and I went into the electricity room.

"We got about... two minutes and forty-five seconds before the cameras cut back on." I told her and we ran down the hallway to the suite we were looking for. Both stopped in our tracks when we heard moaning, I looked at my wife and she looked at me with a disgusted look on her face. Going around the corner I got the surprise of my life. The nigga Johnson was getting fucked by another Spanish man and sucking another man's dick. Bria pulled out her phone and started to record, and I felt sick to my stomach seeing that shit.

"What the fuck!" I yelled making myself known.

All three niggas scrambled to find they clothes, and recognizing the faces of all three men took me out. The nigga getting fucked was Sanchez, Selena bitch ass pops. The other nigga doing the fucking was the bitch ass nigga we was paid to kill by Bria uncle and the other one was the Mayor. The fucking mayor was a booty bandit!

"Wow, look what we have here hubby. Mayor Klerston, Mayor Klerston." She taunted him, and he put his head down while slipping his clothes on.

"When I was told you'll be here at this time, I didn't know you would have company. " I spoke and pointed my gun at Winston.

"Either one of you tell what's about to happen is gonna regret it." Bria said.

"This is for Mr. Luck." she said again and fired two shots killing Winston.

"We won't say anything, I promise you." the mayor cried. I grabbed Sanchez by the shirt and hit him with the butt of my gun knocking him out.

"Give me the keys for this building. You call and get new ones tomorrow. Leave!" I told the mayor and he skedaddled. I tied Sanchez feet and hands together then dialed the clean-up crew. After cleaning up the mess, Bria, myself, and Sanchez left the scene. Dropping my wife off at home, I headed to take Sanchez to the warehouse. Calling up Jamar, I had him in route. I also called Little but I hadn't received an answer from him.

5

JAMAR

I dialed Karter number and it went to voicemail. I knew she cut her phone off or even blocked me. I couldn't even control my temper as I threw a bottle of Remy Martin at the wall and it busted on impact. She ain't know if something was wrong with the kids that she abandoned or not. She left the repass yesterday and ain't been back since! She know all this shit going on and got the nerve to be disappearing. On top of all this shit, Little finally got a call from Jania, and it's not looking good! I'm constantly preparing myself for the worst.

Little been out ever since tearing the city down while I been on fatherly duties cause this bitch wanna leave her kids. This is what I was talking about. I'm currently up at four o'clock in the morning feeding Karson, who couldn't stand my black ass. Every time I come near him, he was crying and throwing a fit. Only time he act right is if Ashtyn grown ass was holding him. Man that little girl is so grown man. She cook, clean, and wash the kids up. She acts as if my kids are her kids. My dukes sent her older friend over to help me with the kids, and I'm grateful for that cause I would've drove myself up the wall continuously here alone. I don't see how my wife do it man. After I got little man down to sleep, I slowly crept out the room.

Ring ring ring!

My phone rang on the dresser, and Mace name flashed across the screen. I thought about ignoring it but on a second thought he probably got a hold to Karter.

"Wassup bro?" I asked and sat down on the bed.

"I got something for you dawg. Meet me at the warehouse, NOW." He told me and hung up.

Since I took over my grandfather's empire, shit been running smooth. Even when I was locked down, shit was gravy. In my prime, I was so ruthless and rough everybody knew not to fuck with me. It was times when niggas was so scared of me I went years without putting my hands on somebody. Now I was dropping niggas like flies! Motherfuckers was gone regret fucking with my family so I was using my connects and reach to get to the bottom of this. My family can't even relax without some shit popping off, and I lost one of the closest people to me. For taking away my brother, everybody had to go, and it wasn't no stopping me. They wanted Jock back and here he is live and in effect.

When I pulled up to the warehouse, Little car was outside and I'm guessing Mace car. I heard grunting and then a smell of probably shit hit me as I walked into the warehouse.

"Aw shit man, you a hard nigga to get in touch with." I boosted as I saw Sanchez tied to a chair. Little was standing over him hitting him in the face. I pulled Little off and Sanchez looked at me.

"Come on, now. I know it was you that called the hit. I know you clicked up with The Haitians and trust me I'm getting them too!" I told him and he spit at my feet.

"Vete a la mierda!" He spat in his Spanish accent and I laughed. I nodded to Little and he started beating his ass.

"This for C!" He said with every hit.

"That's it, that's it." I called out to Little once I saw Sanchez starting to pass out. Little walked to the sink and grabbed the bucket. He threw cold water on Sanchez, and his punk old ass started gasping for air.

"Listen, we can do this the hard way or the easy way. Either way you're gonna die, so either you can suffer or I can make it easy." I told him as Mace hit the light switch and cut the lights on. I'm guessing that's when Sanchez noticed the walls of tools cause he started squirming in his seat.

"I'mma do to you what y'all did to me. Every single day your family gone get a piece of you delivered until you give me every address on everybody you know. I want the names of everybody that's involved, and I also want your wife." I said and his eyes bulged.

"I know she's the one that put you up to this. Our last conversation we had you gave me permission to kill yo daughter, but do yo wife know that? So you around here fucking with me and my family when you gave the order. Maybe I should keep you alive and let your wife know what's going on and maybe she'll kill you herself." I taunted him and laughed.

"Leave my wife alone." He hissed and I laughed.

"Just give me the information, San, and we will be on our way." I told him and he hesitated.

"My daughter has a nine-year-old daughter. Don't kill her, and I'll tell you everything." he said and I looked at Little. Usually, I don't kill women or children but since they touched one of ours nobody was exempt.

"You got my word. Give me names and addresses." I told him and he sighed.

"My phone. It's in my right pocket. Everybody who I work with, including my wife, is in it." He spoke and Mace went to get his phone. It was unlocked and Mace nodded as he went looking through it.

"That's sad you went out like a straight bitch." I said and shot him in the head. I guess Little wasn't satisfied because he emptied his whole clip into San head busting it open like a melon.

"Get into that, and we gone be ready to move out tomorrow." I spoke and turned to call the clean-up crew.

"Bro you good? You heard from Brandon?" Little wondered as we walked out the warehouse. Mace was long gone while Little and I was waiting until the clean-up got done cleaning.

"I'm cool bro. Karter ass dipped out and left me at the crib with the kids so I'm trying to head back there before they wake up. I got so much on my plate from trying to get these bitches to dealing with Karter ass and then my own kids. Man, they not fucking with me and now the Jania shit. I ain't even thinking about Tiera ass. I just hope her ass don't pop back up with no more drama! I still ain't off her ass for getting them people t..."

"You don't even gotta tell me bro." Little said interrupting me.

"We gone get Jania back. I know she ain't dead bro. I feel her in my body." he said and I laughed.

"My shorty strong, but we gotta move out soon though. I know she gone try to call me or something." he said and I nodded.

"But bro, stop stressing, if I'm not stressing about the shit then you shouldn't either. We gone dead all this shit and take our family on a nice ass, long vacation. Also, you gone fix this shit with sis cause you been doing wifey bad bro."

Little said calling me out on my shit. "Nigga you know you been doing her bad ever since this shit came out so don't even play crazy!" he said and I shook my head.

"Man, I just keep thinking if she would have told me it wouldn't have got this bad cause I would've been ended this shit!" I told him and he nodded.

"Okay, she made a mistake. You know sis kind of green to this shit." he told me, and I shrugged.

"Shit can't change now. My brother gone because of this, and we don't know when motherfuckas gone pop up and blast us. Shit, ever since Charles been gone, I can't even think straight." I told him straight up.

"I know how you feel. We lost our shooter and haven't done shit about it. We look like some bitches out here in these streets man, because we ain't even slide for our mans." Little said.

"Well, all that shit over now. Get the crew. We bout to paint the city red behind little brother C." I told him and walked off to my car.

When I got back to the crib, it was a little bit after nine in the morning. I was immediately alarmed when a black Impala pulled up behind me. Automatically in my head, I thought it was an unmarked police car but my hands been clean.

"Jamar Taylor?" the police officer asked and stood with his hands behind his back.

"What's up man? I ain't done shit." I hissed and he handed me an orange envelope. I hesitantly accepted and started to open it.

"You've been served." he said and quickly got into his car and drove off. I angrily laughed as I pulled the papers out of the envelope. This bitch filed for divorce! Walking into the house as I read the papers, what caught me off guard was something about parental rights, and that's when I noticed the house was quiet as hell. Walking up the stairs, I followed the vacuum sound, and Mary, my mother's friend, was vacuuming the kids' room.

"Hey Jamar. Miss Karter just left. She took the kids with her." she said, and I walked over to Kartier closet. It was empty. She filed for divorce and took my kids. Yeah, she was definitely on some get back shit.

6

LITTLE

"FUCK MAN!" I snapped. "Listen, I know she didn't check out so go up to the room while I talk to the manager and check the tapes." I told my nigga Duce. Since shit been going all the way south I had to double up on muscle. I had my nigga from behind the wall send his loyal niggas to me.

"Excuse me, miss, can I talk to the manager?" I asked once the receptionist came to the desk with the room key.

"You're looking at her." She giggled and pulled her hair behind her ear. I pulled out a stack of twenties and slid them across the desk.

"My wife was kidnapped, somebody came and got her from this hotel a few days ago. I wanted to see if you could pull the cameras." I told her and she sighed. She ran her fingers through the money and nodded.

"Follow me." She instructed and I nodded. When we walked to the back, she gave me a remote and turned the camera screen my way.

"Just rewind to the day she was taken and you see her pop up." she told me counting the money. It took me a minute to find Jania on the videos. The cameras faced her until she walked out the lobby talking on her phone. When she walked out, a black truck pulled up, and I paused the video on the dude that stepped out and opened the door for her. I sighed and watched as she got in willingly not knowing it was a trap.

"Can you print this picture out? Is it a way to do that?" I asked and she nodded. She went to the computer, and I texted Mace and Mason in a group chat asking could they get the information on the dude. She gave me the picture of dude, and I snapped it and sent it to the group chat. Everything else can wait because I had to get to my wife soon! On top of her missing, she was pregnant and I had to tell Jamar about her killing Tiera. I ran my hands down my face and sighed. Thanking the lady I gathered my crew and got out of there.

Ring Ring Ring!

"What's up?" I answered.

"How's it going?" Jamar asked.

"Shit, I just left the hotel just now. I only got a picture and I sent it to Mace nem. I'm tryna get some information today and if I get the address I'm sliding." I told him and he sighed. "What's going on with you?" I asked.

"Karter served my ass with the papers and she took the kids." Jamar said sounding sad as hell. I started laughing.

"What, you think that wasn't gone happen? Bro, you been handling sis ass. I wouldn't stay with yo ass either!" I joked and he sighed.

"Fuck you nigga! She ain't have to take my seeds though." He snapped.

"So you don't care about her filing for divorce?" I wondered and he laughed.

"Hell yeah, bitch! She might as well get her money back cause I'm not signing shit!" He said, and I laughed again.

"Man, you fucked up." I told him and he sighed.

"You think sis okay?" He asked.

"Bro, that's yo sister in all but don't ask me shit about her! She tried..."

"Jania nigga!" Jamar said interrupting me.

"Aw yeah, I hope so. I know she cool. I just hope my seed alright to!" I told him.

"Yeah I feel you. I just can't wait until all this shit over. Have you talked to Brandon?" Jamar asked.

"Nah. He won't answer for me." I told him.

"Me either. When you touch down, let me know so you can meet me there." Jamar told me, and I agreed. We chopped it up about the shit we had planned and disconnected the call. Mace sent me an address for one of the dudes who had Jania. It was here in Vegas so I was heading that way now.

When I pulled down the block from the address, I cut the car off. I left the keys in the ignition then stepped out with Duce, Laro and this little nigga name Santana. Santana reminded me so much of Charles with his vicious aim. He was a true fucking beast with the pistol and so I had to bring him on this trip.

"I'mma take Laro. You take Duce. Get the back." I told Santana and he nodded pulling his Automatic out his pants.

"Charles Man." I laughed and headed towards the front porch. Soon as we stepped to the door, I sent my foot crashing to the door causing it to fly off the hinges. Two chicks sprung from the couch and Laro aimed at they heads.

"Sit y'all ass down!" He snapped and they stopped in they tracks.

I ran straight to the rooms with Santana and Duce

checking the back of the house and basement. The first room I walked in it was empty. Checking the other room was a kids' room and the kids was sleep. I walked to the last room and a dude and a chick was sleeping in the bed. I kicked the bed and both of them jumped up. Laro and I had the pistols on them and dude put his hands up in surrender.

"Wake yo bitch ass up lucky charms!" Laro joked and I laughed.

"Man what... Who are y'all?" The dude asked and I laughed.

"Yo worst nightmare nigga! Get up!" I kicked the bed and they both stood up. The chick scrambled to find her clothes but I cracked her with the butt of my gun and she passed out.

"Man, come on man! She pregnant man! Y'all don't gotta do this." His weak ass cried out.

"What's yo name?" I asked and he looked at me. "Marcus." He said and I punched him.

"Fuck man." I grabbed him and Laro grabbed his bitch and we took them into the front room where Santana and Duce already had the two chicks tied up. They started tying the girlfriend up as Laro tied Marcus up.

"You know who I am? You know you and ya mans took a very special package from me a few days ago. Tell me where she is.. Hold up before you start talking." I said as he tried to interrupt me.

"If you tell me you don't know where she is, I'm telling you now, when I'm done with you, I'm killing those pretty little kids in there, your whole entire family, her whole entire family and so on. If you don't tell me, I will find out where she is, dead or alive, and whoever you're working for will get the same treatment. If you do not tell me, I'm going in there, and I'mma make you watch me kill every family member you have. Babies, grandmothers, and all." I told him bending down in his face.

He looked into my eyes, and I saw the tears forming.

"Just don't touch my mama and kids, and I'll tell you everything." He finally said, and I smiled but little did he know his whole family was dying regardless.

"Address?" I asked and he rattled off two address while Santana typed them on his phone.

"They took yo girl back to the second one. I just had inside work here, that's why I got wrapped up." He told me and I nodded. He was bitch made. I didn't even have to touch him, and he was running down the whole operation.

"Where yo phone at? Who you work for?" I asked and he sighed.

"I know somebody named Salt and some Spanish chick. Older lady said you and yo brother had something to do with her daughter getting killed." Marcus said and I nodded.

"Where yo phone?" I asked again.

"In the room on the dresser." He told me and Laro went to the back. I grabbed his phone and shot him three times in the head. I did all the girls like that and went towards the kids room. They all had to go and after I leave here I was heading to his aunt, uncle, and mama's house. I meant what I said when I told him I was gone get everybody!

7
KARTER

The tears were flowing as I looked at the papers scattered across my kitchen table. It's been five months since Charles and Jania been gone and since I filed for divorce. I finally was settled into my new house and my kids were upstairs playing. I haven't seen Jamar since C funeral, and I didn't plan on seeing him. I tried sipping the wine, but I needed something stronger. I threw the glass at the wall, and it shattered getting red wine all over my walls. I smacked the table and swiped the papers to the floor. I couldn't believe after eight fucking years Jamar's trifling ass signed the fucking divorce papers!

I mean, I know I filed, but I thought that would make his ass get his shit together and fight for me! You would think after eight fucking years and five fucking kids later he would fight for his family! He didn't give a fuck; he didn't even try to reach out after I took my kids either or even asked for a explanation why!

"Hey Ms. Karter; are you okay?" Tonya, our nanny, asked.

"I'm fine. Thank you for asking." I smiled weakly and

stood up. "I have to get ready to go. You call me if you need anything." I told her and hugged her.

I walked to the steps and called my kids. They all came running at the same time. Karson was the last one, the smallest little thing, running right behind his brothers and sisters. It seem like Ashtyn hit a growth sprout cause her ass was almost as tall as me.

"Okay, mommy has to run a few places." I told them and the girls sighed.

"We wanna go!" Mariel cried, and Kartier smacked his teeth.

"No, we wanna stay." He said and I sighed.

"You wanna go Jamie?" I asked, and she shook her head no. All my kids were like oil and water. They rarely liked to leave the house. After a few weeks of staying at the hotel, I moved us into our own six beds, four bath house. It was far out from the city, but I liked it like this. Nobody knew where I lived and didn't come all the way out here to mess with me, and I kept my distance. When we finally settled in it seemed like life was better for us.

"Okay, come on Mariel and Ash. The rest of y'all can stay." I told them and they all ran off. I picked up Karson, and he kissed me. He wiggled to get out my arms, and I let him run back up the steps.

"Karson is going to need a nap in about thirty minutes. I'm taking Mariel and Ash with me." I told Tonya and she nodded.

"Okay, I got it under control."

Tonya was a retired nurse that used to watch us when my mother worked at the hospital. She was about sixty years old, but you couldn't even tell. She was a lifesaver and was a huge help around. I grabbed my purse and slipped my feet into my Balenciaga sneakers. My black one-piece hugged my body tightly. I made sure to note that I needed to start getting my clothes bigger. I had a black leather jacket over my one piece with my matching black Chanel purse. I loved rocking all black.

My hair was up in a curly mess at the top of my head. I haven't did anything to my hair since Charles. Nobody was touching my hair unless it was him. It was only April so it was kind of warm out. Ash and Mariel came downstairs, and I thanked God Ash slipped them on something decent. I was too fat to keep up and down the stairs. They had on some matching blue jeans jumpers with some white long-sleeve shirts underneath, and on their feet, they both had on some purple Hunter riding boots. Ashtyn had her purse over her body and glasses at the top of her head. They both had a jacket in their hands. They was my little divas for real.

"Y'all ready?" I asked and they both nodded. The sun was beaming down soon as we stepped out. I hit the unlock on my key fob, and we hopped into my brand new Candy apple red Porsche. I was the only one in the city with this car. After getting it bulletproof and rams customized, it cost me a pretty penny. I barely drive this car cause this was my first baby.

I turned the radio up and hit the code on the gates and they rose up. Yup, my house sat far back behind a steel gate. The only entrance to my house was this front gate. The wall that surrounded my property stood about twenty feet up and it was unclimbable. I absolutely loved this house. Before I moved here, it was a rumor that a very wealthy rockstar built this house, and he died and left it to the state. I was the first person that could afford it so I got it.

Heading towards the city I called my mother but she didn't answer, so I called Mason; he didn't answer either. I started to dial Jania number but caught myself. Man, my girl was really gone. I mean, I don't think she's dead. I just really think the nigga Jason finally got her ass and got her tied up somewhere. Thinking about my bestie had me deeply in my feelings. I was truly missing her and prayed for her and the baby she was carrying were okay.

"You okay Momma?" Ashtyn asked, and I wiped the tears that fell.

"Yes babe. I'm okay. How has school been?" I asked Ashtyn.

"It's cool. Sixth grade is so much different than fifth grade!" Ashtyn smiled, and I laughed.

"I can't wait to go to six grade!" Mariel said from the back seat.

"My babies growing up on me." I told them.

"Ma, can we go get my brother some stuff?" Mariel asked me and I smiled.

"Yes we can, when we leave here." I told them. After about twenty more minutes of driving, we pulled up to the building, then I parked and stood outside the car while I waited for my kids to get out. I had Ashtyn on one side and Mariel on the other.

"Hey, I'm Karter Taylor, and I have an appointment at four o'clock." I told them and looked around the place; it was empty.

"Okay Ms. Karter. He just called you to the back so let's get you in." She told me, and I followed her to the back.

"Afternoon Karter, it's nice to see you." He smiled and I nodded. "Today is the big day. Are you excited?" He asked and I sighed.

"Not really. Girls sit." I told them as they sat down. Ashtyn pulled out her phone and started to record like she always did.

"I'm pretty sure you know the routine already." My

OBGYN said as he pushed the ultrasound machine in the room. Yup, here we are again but this time I was alone. I slipped my jacket off and pulled my straps on my one piece down to my waist. I leaned back on the bed and he squeezed some cold gel on my stomach.

"Okay Karter. What are you wishing for?" Doctor Alston asked.

"A boy." Ashtyn called out, and I laughed.

"Yes a boy. I need to even it out right now. I have three daughters and two sons, so I need one more boy." I told him and he smiled.

"Great choice. Boys are better." He joked.

"Untunt! " Mariel whined and we laughed.

"Okay, here we have it," he said as he moved the nobler around my belly and the heartbeat began to sound. "It's a boy." He continued on to tell me, and Ashtyn jumped up recording.

"Hey guys, as you can see, my mommy is having a boy. Yayyy!" She said recording the screen where the doctor showed the baby.

"Well, baby boy is healthy, and you look like you're measuring about twenty-three weeks and two days. I want you to come back and see me in two weeks." He told me as he wiped the gel off my stomach.

"The desk will give you your sonograms when you finalize a date. See you soon Karter." Doctor Alston said and I smiled. I stood up and fixed my outfit and slipped my jacket back on.

"Yay mommy. I'm happy I got a new brother." Mariel told me and I smiled.

"Me too girl." I told them as the receptionist handed me my envelope.

I set a date for two weeks and left. I dialed my mother again and she answered. It was music playing in the background and the phone hung up. I rolled my eyes and did a U-turn. I was going to her house popping up since she doesn't want to answer. I kind of distanced myself after Charles's funeral. I didn't know how much Charles' death hit me until I was alone in the hotel room and couldn't call him. My whole family was team Jamar so when I left him I left them too. I admit I was wrong for not telling him about the private calls, but he was blowing it out of proportion. He blamed me for Charles' death like I ain't have it hard already. I was fucked up about that and couldn't even have my husband to grieve with. I will forever resent Jamar for not being there for me and our children when we needed him the most.

When I pulled up I wasn't even paying attention to the cars parked outside. I just wanted to see what my mother was ignoring me for this time. Of course the first person my eyes landed on was Jamar, and he was chillin at the table talking. When Mariel and Ashtyn spotted him, they both got excited and yelled "Daddy" and ran to him. His eyes lit up in excitement as he held them tightly. I closed my jacket to hide the baby bump and smiled. I felt a tiny, tiny, tiny bit of guilt for keeping him away from us, but all the guilt went away when a chick stood on the side of Jamar rubbing his shoulder. I know damn well this nigga ain't been fucking around on me. I sighed and walked over there ignoring all the greetings coming my way.

"Who is this?" I asked him. His face softened when he saw me, and I could tell by the way he looked that he missed me as much as I missed him.

"Who the fuck is you?" the girl asked, and that right there told me that he was indeed fucking her.

"Man, chill with all that." He told the chick, and I wanted to smack his ass right then in there.

"Nah, who the fuck is she Jamar?" I yelled again.

"I'm his girlfriend bitch! Who wanna know?" she answered and I looked at him.

"I'm his wife bitch!" I snapped. My mother came out of nowhere standing in the middle of us.

"You let him bring this bitch in here?" I yelled.

"You can tone yo fucking voice down talking to me!" Janet snapped, and I calmed all the way down.

"Ma..." I stopped talking when Jamar whispered in the girl's ear.

"Fuck you Jamar! You want a divorce, YOU GOT IT! Sorry motherfucker!" I snapped grabbing the papers out my purse unaware that I accidentally dropped the ultrasounds out my purse. I threw the papers in his face and turned around.

"Come on y'all!" I yelled at the girls.

"We want daddy." Ashtyn said. I looked up, and my eyes landed on Mariel and Ashtyn who was holding Jamar's hands.

"Give me a hug." I told them and they ran to hug me. I kissed their foreheads and turned to walk out.

"What the fuck!" I heard Jamar yell but I kept going. He was moving dirty out here and fucking off. Fuck him!

"Aye Kar." Jamar called out but I kept walking. When I got to the car, I opened the door but Jamar slammed it back and pushed me to the car and stood over me.

"You carrying my seed and ain't tell me?" He yelled. I smacked my lips and shifted my weight. I avoided eye contact because I know he was pissed off.

"Jamar, get the fuck off me!" I snapped trying to yank my arm but he just held on tighter. He unzipped my jacket and my stomach popped right out. His grip on my arm loosened, and I smacked the shit out of him! "You running around town with bitches now? You don't give a fuck about me! You are not trying to work shit out with me!!" I yelled feeling myself get emotional.

"Look shorty." He sighed.

"It's not that. Karter you know…"

Pow, pow, pow, pow, pow!

Jamar was cut off by gunshots ringing out.

"Jamar! I screamed as he pulled me onto the ground. "Fuck shorty you coo?" He asked and I nodded. I heard the screen door on the house coming open and that's when Little and another dude who I haven't met came out firing at the car. The car sped off as Jamar hopped up returning fire.

"Fuck Kar, you coo?" He asked me again, this time looking all over my body. His hand touched my stomach, and the baby kicked for his first time.

"Fuck man!" He yelled as he helped me off the ground. The family started coming out of the house and Ashtyn and Mariel came running straight to me.

"Mommy! You okay?" Mariel cried as she hugged my legs.

"Yes, I'm good." I told them and sighed.

"Karter, please just talk to me for a second." Jamar begged and I sighed.

"I'm not doing this with you right now, Jamar. You signed those papers so that's what it is." I told him and he shook his head.

"Ma, I didn't sign those papers." He snapped.

"Listen, get home to my kids, and I'll stop by later on. Just let me drop her off." He told me. I shook my head no and opened the driver door.

"NO! Leave her here." I told him and he looked back at

her. The bitch was just standing on the porch as Jamar crew started to get in their cars and move around. The party was over and everybody started to leave.

"Go get in the car girls." Jamar told Mariel and Ashtyn. They looked at me, and I nodded my head yeah. As they walked to Jamar's car, I hopped into my car and left. My head was so fucked up. I thought Jamar would've been handled them and yet here it is five months later and we were just involved in a whole drive by. My head was banging, and I don't even know how I made it home.

I parked in the garage and walked in. Kicking off my shoes by the door I heard my kids laughing and playing in the den. Jamar was on the floor playing with all the kids. Kartier was on his back while he had a kid on each shoulder while Ash was recording them like always.

"Sorry Miss Karter, he just popped up." Tonya said and shrugged.

"It's fine. He's okay." I rolled my eyes and went to the kitchen.

My stomach was growling so I went to the stove to see what Tonya prepared. Lately, my doctor said I was gaining a lot of weight so Tonya had me on this no fried or fatty foods, sweets, pop, juice or bread diet. Only baked meat and water and barely even potatoes. She was starving me and baby J.

"Think you've been doing a good job on your diet so today is a cheat day. I made your favorites because I know you been having a rough week." Tonya said and smiled.

"Thank you dearly. I'm getting ready to smash." I said and we both laughed.

"The kids had baths and ate. I'm going to help them with their homework and put them to bed." She told me.

"I'll help you. Let me eat first." I told her and fixed me a plate.

Tonya cooked some fried party wings, baked spaghetti, garlic bread, and salad. I fixed a big plate of salad and munched on that until my food heated up. I grabbed a water out the fridge and sat down at the table to eat. I was going to let Jamar have his bonding time with his kids since they ain't saw him in a hot minute, but as soon as they went to sleep his ass was out of here! He wanted to play dirty then that's what it was gonna be.

8

JANIA

"You like that shit don't you!" Master grunted in my ear as sweat poured from his body onto mine.

"Shit baby." He moaned and did a few more pumps. I stared off in space as he finished up.

"I see you don't put up a fight no more. I kind of like you better like this." Master said and stood up. I didn't respond. I just stared off into space and did what I have been doing since I got here and that was praying that God took me out of my misery. I don't know how long I have been here but I know it had to be months. Maybe even years, I don't know. I lost count after a month. Soon as they brought me here the rape started. I just prayed they kill me soon! I don't know why they were holding on to me. I have since been moved from the house they held me in. I was now somewhere else, nicer. The place felt like it was closer to...

"Stacey you okay?" He kicked the mattress breaking me out whatever I was thinking about, and I flinched. The beatings was an everyday thing also, and I was surprised I held on this long.

"Yes... Yes..." I stuttered..

"You bleeding Stacey" He said and felt my head. "You burning up? What's wrong?" He asked and sat down by me. I put my hands in between my legs and it was blood all on my fingers. I felt my stomach and the contraction hit me.

"It's time!" I yelled panicking.

"Aw fuck!" He yelled.

Master, as we called him, was an older, Jamaican man. He was handsome but he was older than my daddy. He stood about six feet tall. Master had facial hair that he kept trimmed with some long grey dreads he kept a beanie on. "Max. It's time." He yelled out the door and I was praying they took me to the hospital. Jesus please, if they get me out of here.

"Arggggh!' I screamed out in pain. The contraction hit me harder this time making me stand up as fast as I could. Soon as I stood to my feet the liquid came gushing down like a waterfall.

"Fuck!" Master yelled.

"Sir, you sent everybody home for the night!" Lillian said. Lilian was the maid and the babysitter. We became close over the time I have been here, and we planned on breaking me out but she always would get scared.

"Fuck Lilly." Master walked to me and handed me a blindfold just as a contraction hit me. I bent down until it subsided and slipped the blindfold on.

"You take her to Orlando house while I call the men." He ordered and I sighed. I felt his arms wrap around my arms and he roughly dragged me up the stairs.

"Jania." I heard and Master stopped.

"Shut up bastard !" He spat then I heard a popping sound and it went silent.

"Move!" Master spat and pushed me up the stairs. When we finally got into the car, I pulled my blindfold off.

"Fucck!" I cried out as the contractions started coming faster and faster. "Fuck, please hurry. It's coming!" I cried.

"Fuck. Shit... Shit please. Fuck!"

Lilian started to hit the steering wheel. "Calm down." She screamed. As I paid attention to my surroundings I knew we were going the opposite way of the hospital.

"Please, if you help me I will make sure my family keep you safe." I begged.

"I'm sorry, I can't help you!" She cried out.

"Please. They will kill me and my baby." I begged. She looked at me and then turned around.

"Fuck!" She hissed. "Jania I'm going to help you." she said right before I started to contract again. This time I started to push.

"Please hurry. The baby is coming! I have to push!" I screamed as another contraction ripped through my body. I felt my private area and more blood was coming.

"You're losing a lot of blood Jania." Lilian said and I sighed.

"Please just drive faster. I'm dying!" I cried out. My body started to be weak.

"We here!" She yelled touching my hand. "We made it!" she pulled in front of the entrance and hopped out. She pulled my door open and helped me out of the car.

"Help! She's going in labor. Help!" Lilian yelled, and I stood in the entrance of the emergency entrance.

"Shitttt!" I cried pushing at the same time and this time I heard a popping sound and gave one last push. Lilian caught the baby before it could hit the ground.

"We need doctors!" I heard the man yell before he sat me on the hospital bed with my baby in between my legs. Doctors and nurses rushed to my side while they took me to the back.

"Lilian!" I yelled and she rushed to my side.

"I'm here Jania! I'm here!" She cried. She held my hand as they rushed me and my screaming baby to the back.

"She's going into cardiac arrest." I heard, and everything around me went black.

9

MACE

"We got one more name on the list." Mason said and wrapped his hands up tightly. I did the same as I pulled my guns out cocking them both back.

"I think I'm done with BGF." I told Mason and he looked at me.

"What's wrong?" He asked and I sighed.

"I'm just dealing with my family and shit. I can't do that with me working under y'all and getting into y'all bullshit. It's going on a year and this shit done started back up. I know Jamar and all them still dealing with C murder and extra bullshit with Karter and sis nem but we doing all the work." I told him and looked at Bria. She nodded.

"We done hit up everybody on the list except the ones Little hit in Vegas." I told my little brother and he leaned back in deep thought.

"They fucked up coming after our sister though and if we gotta take the whole fucking state down then that's that!" Mason said and I laughed. Mason was a totally different person from when we first went to college. This nigga done caught his first body and turned into a straight savage!

"Is this about sis nem or C?" I asked calling him out on his shit.

"Whatever nigga! Come on." He snapped and grabbed the handle.

It took us about two months to get at everybody who was in San phone. Our first step was his bitch ass wife but she was nowhere to be found. The last people on the list was some nigga saved as Master and San wife. I thought taking everything that they owned would bring them out of hiding but nope! We tortured they family, wiped out a whole generation of people and nobody came back. The last time anything popped off was three months ago at ma dukes house. That was the final straw for me though. I was making sure I made everybody pay, especially Vanessa, Selena momma, who was the reason for all this!

She put a hit out on Jamar and Karter and when she couldn't get them, she took Tiera, Charles, and Jania. Jania was back home but she was fucked up! They fucked sis up badly. That's why I needed to get to the bottom of all this. At the moment, me, Bria, and Mason was sitting outside of a house. With the help of Lilian, we found the house Jania was first taken to.

"Come on y'all ready?" Bria asked us and we got out. We walked up to the house and Mason was still by the cars.

"Bro, come on. What you on?" I asked him and he smiled.

"I had to do something man, come on!" Mason smirked. Mason went to the back of the house while Bria and I stayed at the front. We counted to three and kicked the doors in. We started firing at everything moving and these niggas was amateurs cause they couldn't even return fire. They was caught off guard and lacking big time! We went from room to room and cleared house. Mason walked to the basement door and flicked the lights. We all went downstairs and it was empty. The basement had a door that led to the outside and it was open. When we got to the door, I could see some dudes running to a truck with somebody chained up. On cue, we all started to shoot but the truck sped off.

"Fuck." I snapped!

"Man, what the fuck!" Mason yelled and I looked back. Bria started to walk around the basement.

"Guys... Run!" She screamed as we heard a ticking sound. I grabbed my wife hand as we dashed out the door. Soon as we got on the outside of the house it blew up in flames causing my body to get thrown across the field. I was in a daze for a second until I heard gunfire. Bria crawled to me trying to snap me back.

"Baby! Bae, are you okay?" She whispered as the gunfire started to get closer.

"Fuck." I groaned and felt the blood trickle down my face.

"Mason?" I yelled out as the gunfire started to get closer to us.

"Fuck man, Mason!" I yelled but he didn't respond.

"Bae, I'm sorry but we gotta go!" Bria screamed helping me up.

I was in such a daze we ducked and ran from bullets as Bria shot back with one hand. My leg and my arm was fucked up. We finally made it to the truck and I hopped into the backseat as Bria hopped into the driver seat backing all the way up as the truck started to shoot at us.

"Damn! Mace, you gotta shoot!" Bria screamed out as bullets start to hit the window.

"Fuck Mace, baby, you gotta shot!" She yelled, but this time she threw her gun at me.

I stuck my arm out the window and started to shoot as she hit the accelerator. It was like a movie man. Bria was driving backwards trying get us away, and I was shooting. My adrenaline was pumping, and I couldn't even feel the pain no more. I grabbed my gun from under the seat and got halfway out the window blowing their front tire. The driver was none other than this bitch Selena. I aimed for the windshield, but the bullets started to bounce off the car. The front tire wasn't enough so I was aiming for every tire. I hit two more tires which made their truck spin out of control. I kept firing until the car flipped and went up in flames. Bria turned around and got the fuck out of dodge.

"Go back! Go back now! We gotta get Mason." I snapped.

"He's fine, baby; he's okay." She shook. "You okay shorty? You good?" I asked calming down.

"Fuck bae!" she snapped. She pulled her phone out the middle console and dialed a number.

"You good man?" She asked. I couldn't hear the other person but she passed me the phone.

"I'm good bro. Get home to the kids. I'll get back with you." Mason voiced.

"Love brother." I told him, and we disconnected the call. I prayed to God that Vanessa and whoever she was with died. I was tired of this shit!

10

MASON

I pulled my phone out of my pocket and pulled up my tracking app. My leg was busted up and my head was bruised, but I was on a mission though. I knew shit wasn't gone go as planned. That's why I put a tracking on the truck before we went inside. I was ending this shit tonight! To be honest, I was done with the BGF family too! I was just waiting until the time was right to tell my fam. After tonight I was ending this shit! Just like Mace, I wanted a family started, too, and I couldn't with all these crazy ass people gunning for us. The first gas station I walked passed, I walked to the first parked car I saw. Luckily for me it still was running. It was a baby in the backseat sleep so I sat the entire car seat on the ground and drove off. I pulled my phone out and followed the GPS. I know it was taking me to the last name on the list.

Master was part of the Haitians and, from what I was told, Marlon's uncle. Since Karter took out Marlon and Selena they clicked up with the cartel and wanted us gone! We was up one though and they couldn't get rid of us! These niggas got lucky by getting Tiera and even Charles, but that's all they was getting from my side! I was taking these niggas out or dying tryin and that's a fact!

Pulling up to the house, it was locked down like Fort Knox! The truck that got away was parked outside, and I sighed then counted five cars and dialed Jamar number. He didn't answer so I dialed Brandon.

"Hello?" he answered coughing and gagging!

"What's going on with you?" I asked.

"Nothing. Nothing bro, what's going on?" He asked, and I could tell by his voice he was going through something. Matter of fact, I haven't even seen him since before Charles died which made me wonder what he was hiding for.

"Hey Brandon. How are you feeling today?" I heard on the other end.

"Let me call you back bro." He said then hung up. I sighed and dialed Karter. She ain't answer so I hesitated. I cocked my pistol back and snuck up to the house. Peeking through the front room window I counted three niggas. I screwed my silencer on and went to the back. I cut the power and I heard commotion going on inside. Peeking around the corner, I saw two dudes come out the front door.

PEW, PEW!

Both the bodies dropped, and I dragged one by one to the side of the house. After a few minutes, another dude came walking out the front door with his flashlight.

PEW!

I shot him in the head like I did his friends and stepped over his body. These niggas was amateurs for real! Ain't no way little ol me could get rid of the whole crew. I heard steps coming from the basement and hid behind the wall.

"Nuke? Tazz? Where y'all niggas at?" I heard as the foot steps got closer. I counted to three and soon as buddy ass came closer I aimed and fired one shot. I heard no movements after a while and went towards the basement. Hearing grunting and coughing caught me in my tracks. Grabbing a lighter out my pocket I flicked it to see what the noise was.

"Ma......Mason?" I heard and dropped the lighter.

"Aw fuck!" I snapped feeling myself get sick.

"Mason? It's me... it's me! Charles." He said and the lights cut on.

11

LITTLE

"How's she's doing?" Karter asked wobbling to sit next to Jania bed. Jania was on the ventilators and couldn't breathe on her own. After she had Jayda, shit went left and she had a heart attack. The doctors got her stable and now it was a waiting game to see when she'll wake up.

"Still the same." I told her and she rolled her eyes.

"Day four…. Were you here when the doctors came in?" She asked and I nodded.

"She's still the same. Just a waiting game." I said and couldn't catch the tears that fell.

"She hung on long enough to give birth. Maybe she's ready to stop fighting." Karter said and I shook my head.

"I can't take that." I told her and she hugged me.

"She hung on to have y'all kid. She's tired and I can tell." Karter said as her eyes got watery.

"I'm not claiming that! She's gonna get up. It ain't over for us." I told her straight up standing up.

"I need some air. I be right back." I told her and walked out. Going upstairs to the NICU to see my baby girl, I stopped when I got to her room. Lily was sitting in the chair, rocking my baby girl Jayda. Jayda is what Jania and I decided to name our baby when she first told me she was pregnant. I knew it was a girl so we thought of girl names.

Just like me, Lily stayed at the hospital day in day out. She wasn't leaving Jania or Jayda side and neither was I. Good thing about everything is the doctors said Jayda would be coming home this week. I was just praying Jania woke up before then. We need her here more than anything. Even though Lily was working for Master in the past I trust her. It was hard to trust her at first, but the stories she told me I knew she was down for my wife. I've grown to love her because if it wasn't for her my wife wouldn't be home right now. I'm still going to keep a close eye on her though. I can't have nothing else happen to nobody else. We have all been through enough!

We already lost Charles, and Brandon was so distant and doing his own thang, so we couldn't take another loss! I still haven't even told Jamar about Jania taking Tiera. I'm not going to say I wasn't hurt at first but all that went out the window when I remembered how foul Tiera had been moving. I even found some shit out about Tiera that I couldn't even believe. Shorty was a snake, and I was glad Jania got her together, or I would have.

The family deserves a vacation and just like Jamar said we were all going on one as soon as Jania woke up and of course Lily was tagging along. Lily was part of the family but Karter wasn't fucking with Lily. Knowing Jania ass, she would kill us if something was to happen to Lily. She saw the best in every situation no matter what it was but don't get me wrong she'll fuck some shit up. She probably only lasted this long because of Lily. Just for that Lily had my respect!

"Hey Little I was just checking on little momma! She so sassy." Lily said and I smirked.

"She got my attitude. I'm about to get some food. Karter up there but I know she is about to be leaving in a few to go get our kids from school." I told Lily and she nodded. I know she would stay here while I go do what I had to do. If I wasn't up here or Karter then I know for sure she would be here.

I went to grab some White Castle since it was right across the street from the hospital. I didn't want to go too far away from Jania in case she woke up. Before starting my car, I prayed. I prayed for Jania recovery, I prayed for our kids, B.G.F, and most importantly my family's strength. We some strong muthafuckas with everything we've endured. I ended my prayer with asking God to please wake Jania up again, I needed her so bad right now.

Waiting in line, I ordered a number two on the menu, which was the two double cheeseburgers, well-done with no pickles or onions, medium, with a grape Hi-C to drink. I made sure to add seasoned salt on the fries with a side of cheese to dip them in. I should've asked Lillian did she want some but I'll be sure to get her a car as an appreciation gift soon as my baby woke up. She was going to wake up soon; she had no fucking choice. When I got back to the hospital, I sat in my car and ate and just walked in with my cup. I took the elevator up to the ICU and when I stepped off the elevator I had this eerie feeling come over me.

When I walked into Jania room she was still sleeping, damn no progress. I was full so I grabbed a cover and settled on the little pull-out bed in the corner and drifted off to sleep.

"Mhmm, Mhmm," I heard but I thought I was tripping. I heard it again and opened my eyes. There she was staring dead at me like she had seen a ghost. I panicked and ran out the room screaming for the nurse. The nurse took her precious time walking to the room as if I was hallucinating about what I was saying. When she walked in she gasped.

"What a remarkable recovery." Nurse McClandon told me. The room swarmed with nurses as they begin to take the tubes out of Jania throat and disconnected her from certain machines.

"Jania honey, can you feel this?" The nurse asked as she tapped her knee, then proceeded to wiggle her toes. She nodded her head yes and then looked over at me and pointed to my cup.

"It's probably watered down ma; it's been a minute." I told her honestly. She insisted with her hand gestures that I give her the cup. I held the straw up to her mouth as she sipped it.

"Damn ma, I'm so happy you're finally awake." I told her kissing her forehead.

"I heard you guys while I was sleeping. Y'all kept me strong and fighting. Where's my kids? Where is everyone?" she said with a very hoarse voice.

"I'm about to call Karter. She went to get them from school. Lily is up there with Jayda. Talk to the nurse for a second." I told her and walked out sending a group text to everyone that she was awake and asking for her family. Karter and the kids arrived in less than twenty minutes; she must've came immediately after grabbing the kids from school.

"How's she doing? You think she's ready to see the kids?" Karter asked before walking into the room.

"Yes, let's go in sis." I responded walking in.

"MOMMY!" Tyaira yelled when seeing Jania which still trips me because she doesn't even ask about her biological momma at all. Even when she first disappeared she still didn't seem too interested. Shit nobody did. I guess everybody was fed up with her shit. Nobody probably cared if she was dead or alive, even Ms. Eva.

All of the kids took turns hugging and kissing her and then our three stayed in bed laying on their mom. Karter and her kids excused themselves to go get lunch and I'm sure to give us some space.

"Um mom, where's the new baby? We want to meet our baby sister." Tyree Jr asked excitedly. Jania smiled weakly and looked at me. The door flung open and Lily, Jamar, Kris and the rest of the family filled the room.

"Sister." Kris smiled hugging Jania tightly. I can see the tears form in Kris eyes while everybody smiled and looked on. As everyone was showing love to Jania the nurse came entering the room with the baby.

"Someone is here to finally meet their mommy." Nurse McClandon said picking the baby up from inside the bed and handing her to Jania. She stared at her for a few seconds before I seen her eyes change and she started to hyperventilate. I walked closer to the bed but was sure not to alarm her that I was aware of her mood change.

"Someone please get this baby away from me! Please!" she yelled damn near just letting the baby drop. Luckily, I was close enough to catch Jayda. Everyone in the room got quiet and was all wondering one thing. What the hell happened to her while she was away?

"Can everyone please step out of the room and give us a moment." the nurse ordered.

"I'll take her Little." Kris offered as she was the last one to walk out. I watched on as the nurse begin checking her fluids and blood pressure. Once everything looked in the clear she pulled aside a chair and got comfortable to speak with Jania.

"What's going on, Jania? What triggered you about the baby?" McClandon asked.

"I don't want to talk about it right now. I just want to enjoy my kids and catch up with them if that's okay with y'all." she said in a nasty tone.

"You got it babe." McClandon said standing up.

"But she is your child Ma." I made sure to add in to remind her ass. All she did was roll her eyes while turning her head to stare out of the window. I followed the nurse out of the room but made sure to not be in earshot with the family.

"What's up with her? She's never acted that way towards our children before." I vented to her.

"I mean she was in pretty bad shape when she was transferred here. Whatever happened to her is causing her to take it out on the child. I'm not a psychologist or anything and if you want her checked out I can send a request in. If she acted like that with a lot of you around there's no telling how she'd act alone with the baby. She could be slipping into Postpartum Depression as well." the nurse told me. I nodded my head thanking her and walked away.

12

JANIA

When everyone walked out the room, Lily came walking back in smiling.

"I'm so happy you're awake." She said hugging me.

"Everyone is in the hallway drooling over Jayda; she's truly the cutest." Lily stated.

"Lily, I couldn't even hold that baby. I don't want to see the baby or even talk about it. Am I wrong?" I asked her honestly.

"Girl, you can feel however you want to feel. Nobody knows what you went through those few months but me. So of course nobody is going to understand but me." she said emphasizing the word me.

I nodded my head because honestly I was done even talking bout that baby. I wanted to cuddle with my kids and my husband but I knew Little's ass was feeling some type of way because Jayda is his seed. He don't know what the fuck I went through every muthafuckin day for those couples of months so fuck him if he wasn't rocking with me! Honestly, who was I kidding? I knew I would never repeat those words to Little. Just maybe if I can talk to him about what I went through he would understand why I'm feeling the way I feel.

I watched as Lily texted away on her phone as if she was arguing with someone. I wondered who she could be texting. She doesn't know anyone here so that was very strange. My eyes were getting heavy so I knew I wouldn't be awake long enough to confront her so for now I'd leave it alone. Before I knew it, I was in a deep sleep having a nightmare about Mister.

∼

"COME ON, just try to see if she latch on or whatever it's called." Little said trying to hand me Jayda. I shook my head no and focused my attention to the T.V. I wasn't paying attention at all but I refused to touch that baby. I tried not to show Little how I truly felt, but he was making it hard pushing this baby on me.

Day three in this hospital, and I was ready to go home. Jayda got discharged yesterday, and I'm glad Lily went home with Little to help him with all the kids plus her. I missed my babies. I couldn't wait to get home so I can love all over them.

"The doctors said I might be able to come home tomorrow." I told Little smiling. He looked at me with a blank expression then slipped a bottle in Jayda's fussy mouth.

"You don't want to feed her?" He asked but I ignored him. The more he pushed this baby on me, the more I hated it. The more I tried to convince myself that something was wrong with me, I hated it. I never felt this way about none of my other kids.

"So did you tell them about Tiera?" I asked Little and he

looked at me. He was about to say something but Karter came around to view.

"What about Tiera?" She asked, and I sighed. Little looked from me to her then licked his lips.

"Uh… Uh." He started to say but Karter sat down and scooted her chair closer to me.

"What about Tiera?" She repeated but this time looking at me. I shook my head and looked at Little.

"I killed her." I whispered and she gasped.

"Bitch, you did for real? When?" She asked not shocked so I was confused.

"The day Charles got kidnapped." I said, and Little shook his head. Karter leaned back and started to smile.

"WOW… I'm not in it. My name Bennett and I ain't in it. Jamar and I is already beefy so I'm not about to be in the middle of more shit. Just act like y'all ain't tell me shit!" She said and I nodded. I shook my head because Karter really changed the subject and act like she didn't know or even care. I knew Little felt awkward at first, but I knew Karter would keep our secret safe. I just don't know how Little was gone tell Jamar or if he would ever tell him. I just hope this secret was kept to our grave.

"She so gorgeous. I can't wait to have this stubborn little boy! Little Jayda is giving me baby fever." Karter said which made me roll my eyes. When I looked up, Little was mugging me.

"Give her to Jania." Little said firmly and I sighed.

"I really don't feel like it. I'm tired and this medicine…" I started to say but Little stood up and walked to Karter.

He reached for Jayda out her arms and she gave her up. I looked at Karter and pleaded with my eyes for her to do something. I wasn't trying to be mean but every time I laid eyes on her it just took me back to a dark place. My mind went everywhere, and I think I started to have a panic attack.

"Jania. Jania!" Little called out to me, but I couldn't speak back. It was like I was there but I was in another zone.

"Go get the nurse!" Little said. He slowly laid me down, and I closed my eyes with the images of the different men that had their way with me.

13

BRANDON

My appetite was finally back, and I was sitting across from Kris digging out. This was the first time I saw her in months and shorty was looking beautiful as ever. She had this glow about her that made me feel like shit because I wasn't the one that was making her happy right now. Thinking about my wife being with somebody else made me sick to my stomach so I set my fork down and leaned back looking at her.

"I'm glad you're finally doing better. I couldn't keep giving the family excuses on why you ain't been around. Nobody has talked to you or nothing." Kris said and I nodded.

"I'm feeling better too! I can go days without thinking about getting high. My appetite finally came back. I ain't ate this much food in months Ma." I told her truthfully and she smirked. I did too because I thought about all the months I have been here and overcame all these obstacles. I was coming up on my nine-month anniversary and that was my release month, then I'll have to do three months out-patient.

"I'm proud of you Brandon. You looking healthy, sounding healthy. What's your goals when you do come home?" Kris asked and I sighed.

Being here put me in a totally different headspace. I wasn't ready to face the reality that Charles was gone, Tiera was gone and Jania just came back. I wasn't ready to face the fact that my brother wasn't here no more! Charles was my boy, and the only thing that kept me going was knowing he would be proud of me but being on the outside and actually not seeing him around the family was gone tear me down.

"You strong Bran. You got through this and did it like a champ! I see the wheels turning in yo head. Don't get discouraged." Kris told me and I nodded.

"I just really wanna see my kids and let them know how much I really really missed and love them." I told her and she nodded.

"Well, I'm glad you're almost finished, and I know the kids miss you dearly." She said and I nodded.

"On a serious note, I have something I want to talk to you about." Kris said which made my stomach turn.

"What's up?" I asked sitting up. I ran my hands down my head and looked at her. I knew it was something deep because she couldn't even look at my face.

"What's up Kris?" I asked again and she bit her lip.

"Okay, so I been seeing this guy... We have had sex and I'm pregnant." She whispered the last part. I smirked because I knew it was a test for her to see how much I have grown.

"For real?" I asked and she sighed.

"Me and him isn't together and we will never be. I understand if you want the divorce now." She told me and pulled out an envelope. She pulled the pictures out the envelope and passed it to me. It was ultrasounds of the baby she was carrying.

Once I scanned over the pictures and made sure it wasn't old, I threw it back towards her.

"Fuck Kris!" I snapped and hit the table. I had to calm myself down by counting to ten cause I almost reached over the table and smacked her dumb ass. "I'm ready to go." I stood up and waved for my therapist to open the door.

"Brandon." Kris called out my name but I kept walking. I think this bitch wanted me to go back to the old me. I had to get far away before I did something or said something I'll regret. I went back to my room and started to pace back and forth.

Ring, Ring, Ring!

"Hello?" I answered. When the automatic woman came on I smiled. Not only was I clean, but I was back talking to my dukes. I ain't really been fucking with her these last couple years just because I was letting the drugs cloud my judgement. Ever since I have been clean, my dukes kept me up.

"Hey Brandon." My momma Brenda voice came through the other side.

"What's up momma?" I replied back and she coughed. "You feeling better?" I asked her.

Since me and my momma been back talking shit was going way smoother in my life. Only thing I missing was my kids and Kris. Kris was on some foul shit though and I wasn't fucking with her.

"Yeah, I'm okay. How are you feeling? How did the visit go?" She asked and I sighed. Outside of Kris, my mother was the only person that knew I was here. I almost slipped up and told Mason but I hung up the phone before he could even ask some questions.

"I'm feeling good. I was having a good time, eating good until Kris came in here with some bullshit!" I told her and she sighed.

"What she do?" She asked and I started to tell her what's been going on with Kris.

I got so carried away with talking to my dukes, about time we got off the phone it was time for my therapist appointment. I was happy somebody my momma hung with got her a new cell phone in there. She was the closest thing I had right now.

When I walked inside the office my therapist Angela was sitting behind her desk. She was typing away on the computer so I sat in the seat I always occupied and got comfortable.

"Hey Brandon, how are you?" She asked and looked up at me. Angela was a beautiful woman. She stood at about five feet six inches and weighed one hundred-and-sixty-five pounds. Angela was White but you can tell she only fucked with the niggas! She was a bad little White broad though.

"I'm fine." I said keeping it short. I ain't wanna tell her what happened with Kris earlier because I was done talking about it. If Kris wanted to be out here giving up her pussy freely then so be it. When I got out of here, I was signing the divorce papers.

"I think it's something you might not be telling me. I can tell by the wrinkles in your forehead." She told me and I laughed.

"I'm good." I told her.

"Well, I'm not gonna force you to talk. As you may know, you're coming up on ninety days. You will be promoted out at ninety then graduate at one twenty. How do you feel that next week you'll be back into the real world?" She asked and I smiled.

"I'm just happy I'll be free! I mean, not free from this place but free from that addiction. I ain't even know how bad it was until I got in this place! I'm just ready to see my kids man." I told her straight up and she smiled.

"I'm glad that you came here, and I love this grown man that's sitting in front of me. I'm glad you've grown, and I'm also happy for you." She told me and I smiled. She had me feeling myself.

"I just wanna give you this homework. Bring this back to me next week. You're dismissed." She told me and handed me a packet. I nodded and went to my dorm. When I walked inside my door was cracked. Rushing inside, I checked and made sure none of my personal items were missing. I kept my room locked up because these people here were thieves! They couldn't wait to get some shit so they could sneak out and get high. We weren't on a twenty-four hour lock down and you could leave if you wanted to. I never left though because I wanted better. I needed to get better for the sake of my loved ones. Grabbing my towel and washcloth off my dresser I went to my bathroom.

In every bedroom it was a full bathroom connected. I'm glad because I don't think I would be able to share bathrooms with any other nigga. Soon as I walked inside, a small baggie on the sink caught my attention. I picked up the baggie and held it up to the light. The powder substance inside was calling my name. I locked my lips and opened the bag. This shit was so addictive but I knew I couldn't go back down this road. Backing up, I went to the toilet and flushed it.

"Great Job Brandon!" Angie said from behind me clapping.

"Congratulations, you have passed your last test." She said and turned and walked away. Only if she knew how hard it was to do that.

14

JAMAR

"Look, I'm not about to have no seed out here by just anybody. I'm sorry shorty but you gotta do it." I told Jessie as we waited for her name to be called.

Jessie was a chick I had been kicking it with for the past few months. I thought we were getting somewhere until Karter popped back up. Now I can't get her little ass out of my head. I mean since I found out she was carrying my son I wanted to be up under her every day. She wasn't fucking with me though. She stuck to her word and signed the papers. When she caught Jessie and I at her madukes' house a while back that put the icing on the cake. If it wasn't about my shorties then she wasn't hearing it.

Speaking of shorties, I had an hour-and-a-half to get my kids from school and the bus stop. It was my weekend and week with the kids so I hope this shit hurry up.

"Is it because you're back on good terms with your wife? I mean, just tell me. She come back around you, you haven't even been fucking with me. You stop answering my calls, coming through, and now this!" Jessie said which made my head hurt.

Shorty ass kept crying about the shit. She knew she ain't want a baby by me. We never even talked about kids and now all of a sudden she wanna have a kid. Keep it real, this ain't shorty first rodeo. Matter of fact this her tenth abortion. She was use to this process, so I don't know why she was acting like she was hurt to do it.

"Look, lose the attitude and don't question me about shit! You acting like this yo first time shorty. Yeah, I got my connects, and I know for a fact you ain't new to this. So chill ma, and be lucky I'm here with you and paying for the shit!" I snapped, and she scoffed and rolled her eyes. The entire time for the rest of the visit Jessie ain't say nothing. After the process, I drove her to Wendy's then dropped her off. I had to do the dash to my kids' school. As I was pulling up they were just letting the younger kids out. Jamie ran with a paper in her hand and came to the front seat. Every time I picked her up she ran to the passenger seat and got in before the big kids came.

"Hey daddy!" She smiled showing a toothless grin. She climbed into the seat and kissed me on the cheek, which she did every time she saw me.

Jamie was a daddy's girl all around. She looked just like my twin except she had Karter's dimples and a mole on her face. She had long, curly hair that Karter kept in two pigtails or a ponytail. Jamie was the sweetest of them all and she was the tomboy.

"How was your day baby girl?" I asked as I gave her her tablet.

"It was fun. We had art class today. Ohh, and we are going on a field trip to the apple orchard. Can you and mommy come please?" She begged.

"Of course. Just let me see when, and I will clear my calendar for you." I told her and she squealed in her seat.

"Thank you daddy!! You the best." She said and had the biggest smile on her face. Mariel came running to the car next. When she saw my truck she started jumping up and down. I stepped out and opened the back door for her to climb in but not before she jumped into my arms hugging me.

"Hey dad! I missed you." She said once she got all the way in. I closed the door and leaned in the window so I could talk to her while I waited for Karter and Ashtyn.

"I missed you too baby girl. You have a good day?" I asked her and she smirked and grabbed her backpack from off her back.

"It's good. I won first place in the drawing contest. So on Monday I get a prize. I get to pick from different prizes too. I mean, I already got everything I want so it's whatever but I still won." She boasted as she showed me the paper.

"Aw shit, okay then, baby girl. We gotta go celebrate tonight! Where y'all wanna go? Skyzone or Bouncetown?" I asked and they both jumped up in they seats. I knew they both were gone get excited. I was happy that I could make them happy.

"Bouncetown!" They both yelled and I smiled. I was just happy that Karter wasn't keeping them away from me. I fucked up royally by pushing Karter and my kids away. At one point of time, I wasn't even acknowledging my kids or treating them right. I wouldn't dare get caught up with anything other than being a father. Being away from them those few little months made me cherish any and every time Karter let me get them.

Kartier came walking down the sidewalk with a group of other young boys. When he saw me he dabbed them up like he was a cool kid and hit his friends with a head nod. I shook my head because although he wasn't biologically mine he acted just like me. The cool demeanor he got from me and just over all, KJ was a cool kid. He was my little homie man and I think we had the closest bond out of everyone.

"Man, pops tell me why I had to stand on some little nigga in the gym today because he tried to take the ball from me." He said and I laughed.

"Man what?" I asked laughing because every single time I picked him up he came with some type of crazy story on how he almost fucked somebody up.

"Man yeah, if I ain't care about getting a whooping by ma I would've beat him up." He told me which made me laugh again.

"Boy, whatever. You not hard!" Mariel said and KJ smacked his lips.

"What I tell you about that?" I asked and he sighed.

"Smacking lips is for girls." He said and looked at me.

KJ looked just like Karter. As he grew older Karter features came right in. He was her twin for real. His swag and attitude was all me though.

"Ohhhh, daddy look at Ashtyn." Jamie called out from the front seat. I looked up and Ashtyn was walking hand in hand with some funny looking boy. When she saw me, she let his hand go. He tried to grab it back but she took off walking fast. When she finally got to me the little nigga kept walking and they waved at each other shyly.

"Who dat little nigga?" I asked her and she rolled her eyes. Ashtyn was stubborn as hell. She didn't fuck with me like the other kids did. She'll let me know in a heartbeat she ain't like me "like that." Ashtyn rolled her eyes and proceeded to put her headphones in. I wanted to grab her little nappy head ass by that weave. She opened the back door and climbed in. I shook my head and went to the driver seat. I called Karter on my way to her house, so I could get Karson then the gang was complete.

"Hello?" She answered on the last ring. She was out of breath and her voice was shaky.

"What's wrong with you?" I asked full alert.

"Shit, Jamar. I think I'm in labor." She said doing a breathing technique in my ear.

"Kar, where you at?" I asked.

"I'm just now pulling to the hospital. Ahhhh shit!" She whined and I stepped on the pedal.

"I'm about to drop the kids off and I'm on my way. Matter of fact, let me call ma dukes nem." I told her and hung up. I dialed Karter right back because she ain't tell me which hospital she was at. After getting to the hospital, I called Janet then my dukes. I didn't even have time to drop the kids off because I ain't wanna miss the birth of my baby boy.

HOLDING my son in my arms was the best feeling in the world. Jamar Charles Taylor was born seven feet, seven ounces on September 1st at 5:27p.m. He has only been here for about five hours and his features was so strong, I couldn't deny him if I wanted to. I know shorty hated me during her whole pregnancy because Jamar was my twin no doubt. I was proud of my wife that she gave me my 3rd biological child.

"Thank you Karter." I whispered and kissed her forehead as she slept peacefully. She stirred in her sleep but didn't wake up. I sat in the rocker chair and laid my son on my bare chest so we could do skin to skin. I covered us with a blanket and leaned the chair back. Soon as we got comfortable my phone started to ring off the hook.

"What's up?" I answered not looking at the screen. I fucked up though because soon as my voice came through the speaker the yelling started.

"So this bitch can have yo fucking baby but I can't? You said y'all wasn't even fucking around! How the hell she have a baby Jamar? I just got an abortion this morning! Fuck!" Jessie snapped and I hung up. I looked up and Karter was looking at me with the nastiest glare. I could see the wheels in her head turn and I prayed silently that Kar ain't hear what Jessie said. I couldn't afford my wife getting mad about some shit that happened when we were split!

Don't get me wrong, thinking back, I handled shit all the way wrong. Karter ain't did nothing but proved to me how loyal and down she was for me. As soon as some shit I couldn't handle popped off and shit got real, I folded.

"So let me ask you." Karter said sitting up. I sighed and sat up also. I already know shit about to go left. I stood up and handed baby Jamar to Kar. I went to the drawer they kept his clothes in and got a diaper, wipes, and onesie out for Karter. After getting all his stuff together I went and slipped on my shirt and slides.

"So where are you about to go?" She asked laying the baby in between her legs as she got him settled.

"I'm just about to go. I don't want to argue with you Karter and I'm not about to." I told her straight up and she looked at me.

"Wow Jamar, are you serious? I'm so sick of the shit you say to me and the way you handle me!" She started to say as the tears threatened to fall. I kind of felt bad. "You don't even know how bad you are hurting me which is the bad part. It's not fair to me hearing some bitch talk about being pregnant by you!" She yelled and the tears started to fall. "You out here running wild with different bitches. You didn't see the kids or me in five fucking months and you can just move on? That's fucked up for real." She started saying again, but by this time the tears were flowing.

"I'm so hurt! You hurt me so bad and I gotta suck it up and pull my big girl panties on." She added. I sat on the side of the bed and pulled her into me as she cried into my chest.

"I'm sorry Kar." I told her straight up. It wasn't nothing else for me to say; the damage was already done.

"You said you didn't sign the papers so who did?" Karter asked and I sighed. I ain't wanna tell her that Jessie signed them and sent them to her because I didn't want her to know how serious Jessie and I *WERE*. To be honest, I knew where Karter moved to when she moved. I had my people watching her house on a daily basis. I just couldn't look at her face without thinking about C. Since she had my son someway I felt God was putting Charles back with us through my son.

"I don't know. Not me." I said and she sighed.

Knock Knock Knock!

Kris, Mason, and Janet walked in. They had balloons and gift bags.

"Whew, bout time y'all made up! I missed the gang." Kris said which made me laugh. She came right in and washed her hands so she could hold baby J. I stood up and hugged Janet then Mason and sat back down next to Karter.

"He's handsome you guys." Janet said as she looked at the baby over Kris shoulder. I put my arm around Karter and she leaned on me. I was just happy that she let me this close to her.

∼

"Mommy's trying to sleep." I whispered as I held the baby in my hands.

Karson was crying for me to pick him up and the rest of the kids were jumping off the walls. Ashtyn was laying across the couch typing away on her phone, and Mariel and Jamie was fighting each other. Kartier was jumping from couch to couch, and I just got the baby to sleep.

"Alright sit down." I told Kartier and he sat down.

Mariel and Jamie went to opposite couches and I sat down. Exhaustion wasn't the word for me. It seemed like all Karter did was sleep since she been home. I tried to come over every day to help her with the kids but they were tiring me out.

"Dad, are you and mommy back together?" Mariel asked and Ashtyn smacked her lips.

"You know they not. Dad just here because she had the baby. He'll be gone soon!" Ashtyn grown ass said and rolled her eyes. She walked away typing on her phone. I turned the TV on but the words my oldest had just said to me kept replaying in my head. I'm going to try and have a talk with her because when she came with us she loved me and now she hated me. I don't understand where I went wrong. Once I settled Karson and got him to sleep I went and checked on Mariel and Jaime and they were chilling in their room watching *Frozen* on DVD. Going to check on Kartier, he was in his room watching *Criminal Minds*. He got such an old soul; he loved all the old school movies and TV shows. Finally going to have a talk with Ash and approaching her room I heard her on the phone.

"But listen, who does he think he is? He can't come and

go as he pleases. That's just not how life works." Ashtyn told whoever was on the phone.

"I'm not trying to hear it's no grown folks' problem. He didn't hear my mommy when she was in there crying her eyes out every night silently thinking we didn't hear her," she continued.

"And on top of that, she's not even my real mom so he basically just threw her to the wolves with me and I still never once heard her complain since the day she brought me home with them from the hospital."

It kind of hurt me to know she understood what was going on and from this day forward I knew I had to do better for the sake of my family. Knocking on the door she immediately yelled, "Go away!"

"Just five minutes Ash, please." I begged her.

"Let me call you back later. Come in Dad." she told me.

"Whatever you got to say you don't even have five minutes. You have three so let's please talk so I can study." she told me but before I could start she interrupted me.

"Wait, let me go first. Oh, and don't worry. Your three minutes don't start until I am finished with what I got to say." she told me. She amazes me even when she's back talking.

"Go ahead Ash, it's your world baby." I told her.

"I just want to say that it's not fair that you get to come and go when you please. Do you know how many nights mommy has sat in her room and cried because of you not being here with us? That's why I help because I know mommy gets tired when we are here alone. I could've calmed the kids down earlier but since you're here I gave you the honors. I already don't have my mom and then you just be disappearing," her voice started to crack as she continued.

"Mommy Karter has never gave up on me. She has never let me down. She has never left me, none of that. I might only just bout to be a teenager but growing up with my other mom I had no choice but to grow up before my time. Kar lets me be the kid I want to be even with me helping out with the kids. I miss you daddy." she told me now in full blown tears.

I walked up to hug her and surprisingly she let me. I let a few tears drop myself because if this was how my twelve year old daughter felt I can only imagine how my wife felt. Well, ex-wife. Once we wrapped our conversation up, I was headed out the room to go wake up Karter and get my family back in order. I bumped right into her walking out of Ashtyn room and she was trying to hurry up and wipe her tears.

"Hey sorry. I was coming to check on all the kids but you guys were talking. Let me say goodnight to my baby." she told me walking into the room and leaving the door cracked.

"Ash, I never knew you heard me up crying those nights. I don't ever want you to feel a certain way about your dad. I'mma make sure that fool do better towards y'all. I love you, baby girl, and we turning up this weekend so be ready." Karter told Ashtyn kissing her on the forehead as they both laughed.

"Goodnight and don't be on that phone all night Ash." Karter told her walking out of her room while flipping the light off and shutting the door.

No words were exchanged as I followed her to her bedroom and watched her strip and climb into bed.

"Jamar, you only have one time to lie during this conversation and I'm done with you." Karter began.

"Alright Karter, what's up? What you want to know?" I

asked her dreading to answer any of her questions. Knowing Karter she already knew everything that was going on.

"How in the fuck did you slip up and get this bitch pregnant Jock? How would you feel if I was pregnant by another nigga." she yelled.

"Listen, I didn't mean to get her pregnant shorty and stop yelling. You know the kids can hear us. Plus I know Junior is mines; the nigga look just like me ma!" I told her.

"Okay, I said what if I was to be out here pregnant by somebody else. How would you feel?" she repeated herself.

"What you mean ma? You know how I would react! I'll fuck around and kill you, him, and the baby!" I stated firmly. I meant everything I said too.

"EXACTLY MUTHAFUCKA! So it's cool if I kill you and your little bitch right?" she asked.

"Nah, see the baby is already gone. I'm done with that Kar. I wanna come back home."

"Who the fuck signed them divorce papers if you didn't Jock?" she asked.

"She did." I said lowly.

"Come again, say what? Don't be silent now. Speak the fuck up." she told me.

"Watch your tone Karter." I warned her.

"Nigga, I ain't gotta watch shit. What did you just say?" she asked me again.

"She signed them Karter damn." I admitted.

"Get out." she stated.

"What the fuck man. You told me be honest." I sighed.

"Don't make me repeat myself. If it ain't about the kids you have nothing else to say to me bro. I'm done." she told me. I felt like somebody kicked me in my chest with some Timberland boots on. I watched as she slid down under her covers and turned over. Yeah she was done with this conversation and I'd leave it alone... for now anyway.

My phone began to ring as I was walking out, and I didn't even bother to answer it. It vibrated a few minutes after it stopped ringing indicating a text. It was about business and I told them to call Little. I was off for a couple days. I had to get my family back; I couldn't do this.

15

CHARLES

"Help us get close to them and we'll let you live." He said and hit me. I was fucked up badly and couldn't defend myself right now while he taunted me.

"You might as well just kill me then because I'll never switch up!" I said with the little bit of breath I could muster up. They had been beating my ass since I got here, and I still ain't told them shit. I wasn't no rat and definitely not about the family. I know they were painting the city red looking for me as we speak.

"He a tough one boss, but we knew that so what we do next?" One of Mister workers asked him. Mister was Marlon bitch ass uncle, real name Marley. I only know because he was one of the few we did business with a while back. Only if he knew he fucked up majorly by fucking with us! Even if I don't make it out of here I know my people go hunt them down!

"Cut his finger off and deliver it to the family." Mister said as he got up from his seat and walked out with some old Mexican bitch.

"It ain't over. SEE YOU IN HELL PUSSY!" I spat before a dude cracked me with something knocking me out.

"C, Charles man." Mason shook me waking me up. I was

having the same nightmare every single day since Mason saved me.

"I'm up. I'm good." I said and stood up.

Mason went to the back, and I went to the bathroom. Standing in front of the mirror my reflection scared me. I wasn't the same Charles; this Charles staring back at me scared me. I had permanent scars on my face from getting beaten with chains and sticks. I had a permanent limp when I walked from my left leg getting broken so many times. My head had a dent in the middle; they fucked me up. I was a different Charles, but I was a stronger Charles, and that's what scares me. Stepping into the steaming hot shower, I scrubbed my body to get the traumatizing smells off me.

Being locked up and tortured did something to my mental. Raped, beaten, degraded, I knew it was only my karma for the fucked up shit I did. My skin was red when I got out from the hot water. After drying off, I wrapped into my towel and went to the room Mason had me housed in.

Mason literally was a gift from God. Just as I was giving up and stopped fighting, he came and saved me. When he told me everybody thought I was dead, it crushed the little bit of hope I had left in me. He also told me the family was going through it and mourning me which brought comfort to my heart.

This whole six weeks Mason nursed me back to health. I had my strength and mind was back. Most of all, my sanity was returning! I wasn't giving Mister or Vanessa, Selena momma, no more of myself. Next time they entered my mind, it was gonna be when I kill them.

Stepping into my grey sweatpants, I slipped my feet into my slides. I grabbed my shirt and slipped it on as I walked out of the bedroom.

"Yeah, I'll be there tomorrow. I have just been having

some shit to take care of. I know, sis. I'm sorry; you know I got you." Mason said, and I sat down on the couch.

He held his finger up for me and I nodded. I knew he was talking to Karter and my heart broke. I missed out on so much time, and I can't wait to see everybody so I can just hug and love all on them. Especially my boo Karter! I missed her more than I missed anybody. After Mason wrapped up his conversation, he scooted to the end of the couch.

"It's time for you to come out." Mason said and I sighed. I was ready on the outside but on the inside I don't know how I'd react.

"It's time." Mason said and stood up. "I'm about to head out, but I'mma be back in the morning because we meeting up at Karter shit." Mason said then grabbed his keys.

I shook my head and went downstairs to his workout room. This room was my therapy, and to erase all the bad energy and memories out my mind, I busied myself here. Putting on my headphones, all I thought about was going hard and getting strong. I ain't have time to play; everything was about to change tomorrow when my feet touched the pavement.

16

KRIS

"I'm not about to do this with you Marcel. If you don't want me to have this baby then okay fine, but I'm not getting an abortion and my husband knows." I snapped feeling like throwing up.

Yeah, I fucked up by fucking with Marcel. He was one of the closest people on BGF side. He worked under my husband, and was there for me when Brandon couldn't be.

Marcel and I started messing around right after Charles' funeral. He was Jamar's driver but since Bran had to leave Jamar sent him to drive for me. That's when shit went downhill. Look at me, caught up by the runner when I was fucking with the boss!

"You told him?" Marcel asked sounding like a girl.

I mean Marcel had bitch tendencies, and I don't even know how I made it this far fucking with him. All he did was complain. He had great dick though, and that's what had me hooked from the first time.

"Yes, I told him I was pregnant, but I didn't tell him by who, because you would've been dead a few days ago. I'm telling you now though if you try any of that bullshit you been on when Bran come back you'll be canceled!" I told him straight up, and he smacked his lips.

See, bitch shit. I haven't told anybody where Brandon was. Shid, everybody just thought he went MIA cause of Charles' death. Nope, he had to get to rehab when I found his ass passed out in my bathroom, overdosing.

"You foul Kris." Marcel cry baby ass said which made me roll my eyes. Everything this nigga did pissed my life off.

"You foul nigga. You want me to get rid of my seed because you don't want yo bitch to know you was cheating. Boy, fuck you!" I snapped. On top of this nigga being a bitch, he had a bitch which he lied and said he was broken up with. Come to find out shorty ass was five months pregnant also.

"Look, I'm offering you the money to get an abortion. Yo nigga ain't about to raise another motherfucker baby, and my girl ain't accepting no outside babies." He said which made me laugh.

"Nigga, okay; just keep yo mouth shut and nobody will fucking know you the daddy because I surely don't need you!" I snapped and hung up the phone.

I wasn't mad at Marcel at all. I knew when I found out he had a girl shit could go either way. I was prepared to raise my baby alone. I did it with all my kids before. Marcel wasn't saying nothing I ain't already heard. Rolling over in bed as my alarm went off, I sighed because this nigga fucked up my morning. I have been arguing with his ass for the last two hours when I really should've been getting some sleep.

Braylon and Britton came into the room and climbed into the bed with me.

"Good morning, mommy; we wake up." Britton's little voice said which caused me to smile. Britton and Braylon was always the first to wake up. Britton said the same thing every morning. This was my daily routine.

"Good morning babies. You girls ready for y'all big day?" I asked sitting up.

As soon as I sat up, my baby started to move. I sighed and thought about the way Brandon acted when I told him about the baby. I been texting and calling since, but he ain't answered and he even denied the visit. That's until last night he called me and told me to bring the girls over Jamar house. They all were meeting over there to discuss where we are going for Karter's birthday this year. I guess since the beef shit done died down, shit was slowly getting back to normal. I couldn't wait for my girls to see they daddy face though. I just hope the rest of today goes smooth.

"Yesss." Braylon screamed and I stood up.

Soon as I stepped foot on the ground, I felt sick. Making it to the toilet, I threw up whatever came out which was nothing. This little demon seed inside me been giving me hell for the last four months.

"Mommy, you okay?" Brylynn asked wiping the sleep out her eyes.

"Yes, mommy is fine. We going to get breakfast this morning. So let's go get dressed." I told my girls as I went to the extra room where I kept their clothes.

Picking out them the same outfits like always, I brushed their teeth, washed their faces, and slipped their clothes on.

"Go find y'all shoes while I shower right quick." I told them and they ran off.

I went straight to my bathroom and brushed my teeth then gargling mouthwash afterwards.. Stepping into the shower, the hot water ran down my body. Washing my body then stepping out ,I dried off and oiled my body down. Slipping on my panties and bra, the girls came into the room fully dressed with they shoes and jackets on.

"Okay, I'm almost ready." I told them and they sat on my bed. I slipped on some black ripped up jeans from Fashion Nova with a black Jean jacket to match.

"You look pretty mommy." Braylon complimented me and I smirked.

I was at the time of my pregnancy where I felt ugly. I was getting fatter and fatter and only thing good was the glow.

"Thank you baby." I smiled and slipped my feet into some black Balenciaga's; the ones that look like socks. I stood in the mirror and took my bonnet off, and my silky hair fell down in place.

"Let's go." I told them as I gathered all our stuff to leave. Our first stop once we got into the car was this place called His Eatery to get breakfast. After eating, we headed to Karter house. We were meeting at her house because she had my nephew and couldn't leave out the house yet.

"Mommy, are we going to Tete Karters?" Braylon asked me.

"Yes we are. I have a surprise for y'all." I told them, and they got geeked in the back seat. I turned the music up and started to think about how Brandon was gone act towards me since the last visit didn't go well.

When we pulled up to Karter's, I thought we'd be the first to come, but it was cars parked around her driveway. My sis moved into a nice ass house after her and Jamar split. It was huge, and I was proud of the woman my little sister had become.

After I parked and got my kids out, I walked inside, and we kicked our shoes off at the door. I went in search of the family as the girls went towards the stairs to go down to the game room. Walking into the kitchen, Karter had the baby in front of her in the carrier as she busied herself.

"Hey sis." I spoke as I sat in the chair on the island.

Karter looked back at me then rolled her eyes.

"Don't hey sis me. I'm not fucking with you!" Karter said and I sighed. It was always something with this family.

"What I do now?" I asked.

"You pregnant and ain't tell me." Karter said and rolled her eyes.

"Whew, child. Aight, I'mma head out." I told her and laughed as I stood up.

"Where everybody at?" I asked and grabbed a bottle of water out the fridge.

"In the den. Take this in there." She said and handed me a bowl of chips. I grabbed my purse and went through the front room; the whole family was in the den but looking through the front bay windows, what caught my attention made me scared shitless.

"Charles?" I all but yelled and his smile spread wide as Mason opened the door for him to come inside. "On my god! CHARLES." I screamed and that's when I heard all the family coming to the front room.

17

KARTER

"Charles!" I heard Kris yell and dropped the cake on the counter.

"Fuck!" I snapped as Baby Jamar started to whine.

I shook my head and started walking towards the commotion in the foyer of my house. Kris was yelling and when I rounded the corner Charles was standing there, smiling. I mean Charles for real. He was here in the flesh. At first, I thought I was dreaming but I wasn't. C was really here!

"What's up sis?" He said and turned to me.

The tears instantly came to my eyes, and we walked to each other. Time must've stood still because all I saw was C. Everything played back in my mind. C's death, the funeral these past few months, none of that mattered though. Charles was here in the flesh.

"Charles. Oh my god!" I cried as he hugged me. Kris had to come get Baby J because I wouldn't let him go. It felt so unreal. I was scared that if I let him go he would disappear. I had read so many urban books about somebody loved ones dying and then coming back and prayed this was the scenario. C was back in real fucking life!

"Man, I missed y'all so much!" Charles deep voice said and I couldn't stop smiling.

"Hold up, hold up. This nigga was just dead... This ain't suspect?" Kris said which made everybody laugh. I mean, it was weird, because if he was here who did we bury? Who body was burned up like that? I held up Charles hand and his finger was missing. I put my hand over my mouth, taking a good look at him. It was all different types of marks and scars over his face. I couldn't imagine what type of pain and torture he been through.

"Explain please..." I finally said and he nodded. He walked up to Jamar who haven't said anything at all. Charles put his hand out for Jamar to shake and Jamar grabbed Charles and hugged him. I could tell by the way Jamar was breathing that he was shedding tears. Happy tears of course! It took us a lot to bury Charles or whoever it was. Him standing in front of us was not only shocking but scary.

∼

"Yeah, I was the one that saw you that night they brought you. I was already fucked up and had no fight in me." He told Jania after he explained everything he has been through. I mean, it wasn't a dry face in the room at what he revealed to us!

"When Mason came in the house, they came down to kill me but thought I was dead. I couldn't move, my ribs was broken so I couldn't really breathe. They just assumed I was dead I guess." Charles said. After he told us what's been going on and how he has been getting tortured these past few months, really the entire year and some change, we all were was just standing around shocked. The kids were even confused about the whole situation.

Once the confusion faded, they were all as happy as I am! Especially Kartier and Ashtyn. They ain't even want him to leave because they were scared they wouldn't see him again. "Everything y'all was doing out here I know about. They told me about how y'all went to Jamaica and killed Marlon's family. Sanchez is dead. I know about it all. Y'all thought Vanessa and Mister was dead but they're not! That night or whatever happened, they got free and escaped the car before it blew up." Charles also said and I was confused now. Mace stood up and so did Mason. I knew that what he was saying now only them two knew what he was talking about.

"I do know that they are the only two left. Y'all done wiped out the whole family's existence." Charles said and looked at Jamar.

"I also know y'all didn't stop looking for me! I know y'all did what y'all had to do." He said to Jamar especially.

"So Mason saved you?" Kris asked and looked between the two. I guess trying to figure out something but I just shook my head.

"Uh, where is Brandon and Tiera?" Charles said and I sighed. I didn't know where Bran was but Tiera, we would never see her again. She was indeed dead.

"Well since we bringing surprises up, I have another surprise for you guys." Kris said typing away on her phone. She walked away and when I heard the door open and shut, I heard her yell for her kids to come downstairs. Kris came in with Brandon following after, and it was definitely a celebration for us. I couldn't even be mad about nothing, I was just happy the family was back complete.

. . .

Few days later...

"Hey, I'm Karter Taylor. I'm here for my son's six week checkup." I spoke to the nurse at the counter. She typed at the computer then told me to sign in and sit down.

Ring Ring Ring.

"Hello?" I answered and it was silent.

"Hello?" I asked again and Jania's voice came over the speaker.

"What are you doing?" She asked cheerfully, which was surprising to me. Ever since Jania came home shit been rocky for her. She was going through postpartum depression, and I felt bad for my girl. She didn't have a strong mind, and I hated for her to go through what she went through.

"Nothing, I'm watching T.V. How are you feeling?" I asked and crossed my legs over at the knees.

"I could be better. Are you still picking up this little baby when you leave there?" She asked and I smacked my lips.

"Girl, have you been trying to bond with Jayda or not?" I asked. I started to pick Baby Jamar up but the doctors called my name.

"Just be here please. I have to go. Okay bye." She said and hung up. I shook my head as I struggled to carry the baby, diaper bag plus my purse.

"How are you and Baby Jamar?" He asked and I smiled.

"We are fine actually. This little guy is big! He makes my back hurt carrying him." I laughed as the nurse typed away on her tablet.

Knock Knock Knock!

"Come in." Nurse Kelly said and Charles walked in. He called me earlier and told me he was coming to the appointment with me because Jamar had to go handle something else.

"Hey C." I smiled and he hugged me. He grabbed Jamar out my hands and sat on the clinic bed.

"Okay, he seems good; the doctor should be in in a minute." Nurse Kelly spoke and walked out.

"So how was your morning today?" Charles asked and made a funny face. I laughed and stood up. I had to stretch my legs because lately I have been feeling more tired than usual.

"What's that face for?" I smirked and he smacked his lips. I rolled my eyes and he did also.

"So Jamar spent a night last night?" He asked and I laughed.

"Boy, first of all, he stayed until like two this morning and he didn't sleep in the room with me. He stayed on the couch." I told him and he puckered his lips up.

"Don't play with me! You thought I was playing when I said Jamar and I split." I told him. After the last talk with Jamar, nothing changed. He kept trying but I just wasn't feeling him. Charles and I was right back close like nothing ever happened. If we weren't with each other once a day we would be on the phone with each other all day long. That was my nigga, and I was happy he was back. Shit Jania wasn't fucking with me like that. She had Lily. Kris and Brandon was back like crack addicts so I had C, which was fine with me.

"Well, we about to get y'all back right! I can't have my fave people beefing!" Charles said which made me smile.

"I was contemplating on telling Jamar that Tiera was working with Mister and Sanchez." Charles said and my stomach dropped. I put it in the back of my head about what Jania told me what happened to Tiera. Jania knows me and knew I wouldn't tell her secret.

"I think you should tell him. They are probably the ones that got Tiera. She just disappeared out of nowhere." I said and Charles nodded.

"So how have you been feeling though?" I asked genuinely concerned. I can tell just by looking in Charles; face; he was a different person. I'm not sure if it was for the bad or good but C wasn't the same.

"I'm good. I just thought it was gone feel awkward being back. Y'all missed me as much as I missed y'all." He told me and I nodded. I stood up and hugged him.

"So why couldn't Jamar come again?" I asked and we both laughed.

I may have put on the act that I was over Jamar, but Jamar had my heart and he knew it. I just wish we could've got our shit together. My kids missed him and so did I.

"He said he had something to do this morning. I'm not sure. Let's talk about this trip." Charles said and smirked.

Every year around my birthday we all went somewhere out of the state. With everything we done been through this last year, everybody was looking forward to this vacation! This year the BGF was taking over Dubai. Jamar and I been twice but every single time we went it was perfect. Plus we never took the kids with us, so this time they were going. I couldn't wait either.

"I need to go shopping by the way... When we leaving?" I asked as the doctor came in the room.

"Hello Miss Karter. How have you been?" Doctor Galston said as he took baby Jamar out of Charles' hand.

"This isn't Jamar. Who may you be?" He asked and I laughed.

"This is my brother, Charles. Remember I told you about

him." I told him and he nodded. He smiled and shook Charles' hand.

"Nice to meet you. Now let's look at little man for you." He said and started to check on baby Jamar.

After the visit, Charles followed me to the mall so we could do some last minute shopping for our trip.

18

MACE

"We gone sit back there." I told Bria as she carried our baby girl. We were the first to get to the private plane Jamar, Little and myself rented for our trip.

"That's cool with me. I hope this vacation is drama free and nothing but good vibes." Bria said as she sat our baby girl Brielle in the seat in the middle. Montana was with Karter, and they haven't arrived yet. I know she was gone be the last to get here.

"We are not talking about anything that pertains to business on this family vacation." Bria said and I nodded. I smiled because this was really the first time we had a break from the world since our honeymoon. I wanted to drop another baby in my wife before we headed back home.

"Good morning family!" Kris said as she walked up the steps with her kids and Brandon in tow. She tried to keep it a secret that Brandon was in rehab, but I knew all along. I ain't speak on it because it ain't my business but I been around drug addicts all my life. I knew Bran was on that shit. Everybody else just played crazy.

"What's up y'all. Good morning." I spoke and so did Bria.

"Hi, uncle Mace and TeTe Bria." Braylon spoke and hugged us. They sat in between Brandon and Kris right in front of us. The next set of people was Mason and Charles. Since Mason saved C, they had been really close. Mason trained Charles and got him back strong and aim back right, and I guess they been combined at the hip since.

After a good half hour, the rest of the crew started filing in. Of course everybody sat with they family. I was just hoping like Bria said this trip was drama free.

～

WE WERE in the air for seventeen hours and most of the time we slept. The kids was up getting restless from being on the plane so when we landed the first thing we all did was go to the house Jamar had rented.

The house we were staying in set on the beach of course but it was huge.

"Damn bro! How many rooms this bitch got?" Little said and Jamar smiled. He shook up with Brandon and then Charles and Karter took off running to the house.

"I got dibs on the first room!" She yelled and Kris ran after her.

"I'm second." Kris yelled.

"This is nice son. I'm proud of you." I heard Eva say and hug Jamar. I grabbed Brielle from Bria's arms and we went inside. We went down the stairs and found the kids' rooms; it was five rooms downstairs all with kid colors and decorations.

"This can be Montana and Brielle room then." I told her as Montana went inside and started pulling some toys and stuff out that was already here. Bria let Brielle down and she walked off following her brother.

"Let's go see what we got planned for the day." Bria said as the rest of the kids came running down the stairs followed by Ms. Tonya, Karter's nanny.

"I got the kids. You guys go and enjoy yourselves." She said and we went upstairs to find us a room.

After everybody got settled in, the women went into the kitchen to cook while we went on the back dock and watched the kids play.

"How you feeling little bro?" I asked Mason as he sat next to me. He had his drink in one hand, while we all just chilled.

"I'm good. All is well!" He said and Charles sat next to him. They started to indulge in their own conversation, while I chilled and vibed out. A few minutes later, the woman came out with the food and sat the kids down to eat.

"I'mma say grace before you hungry ass niggas start eating." Eva said and we all stood up.

"Father God, I do not come to you to ask you for anything because you gave us a lot, Father. I simply speak to you to say thank you Lord. Thank you for being so good to me and my family, thank you for bringing my son Charles home to us! Thank you, Lord, for wrapping your arms around us all and giving us this great life. Continue to watch over us and bless the food we are all about to receive. In your name we pray, Amen!" Eva prayed, and we said Amen in unison and sat down.

"So tonight is the men night!" Jamar spoke.

"Tonight, the guys are gonna go out and leave the women here. Tomorrow the women are gonna get up, go shopping, pamper themselves for us men to take them out tomorrow night. Sunday, family day, where I have a whole day planned for us, and Monday... is a special day." Jamar spoke giving us the rundown on what we were doing for the next four days.

"You better be on your best behavior. I would hate to have to leave you here." Karter told Jamar and everybody laughed.

"What Karter said!" Bria agreed which made me laugh.

"So fellas, we leaving here about 10, the car leaving at 10:20, so if y'all not down by then y'all getting left." Jamar spoke, and we all just finished eating having casual conversation.

19

MASON

"I'm just glad you got me out that bitch!" Charles said and passed me the blunt he was smoking. I took a pull from it and passed it to Mace. We were all chilling on the dock before we got ready to go out. The women took the kids to the beach so it was just us fellas at the crib now.

"Watch the ladies try to crash our men night." Jamar laughed.

"That's why we tell them we are going to one club and go to another one." Little said and I dabbed him up.

"Good thinking bro." Brandon said. He hasn't really said too much since we have been here, and I wondered why that was.

"I'm about to gone head and get dressed." Charles said and stood up. He grabbed his phone off the table and headed into the house. I fixed me another drink before I excused myself and went to get dressed.

Stepping out of the shower, I wrapped the towel around my body and slipped my slides on. I let my body air dry as I oiled myself down. Sitting on the bed, I hesitated on getting dressed first.

Knock Knock knock!

"Come in." I said as I walked to my dresser and grabbed the pre-rolled blunt. Karter came in with a cup in her hand and sat down smiling. I can tell she was tipsy.

"Hey, you okay?" She asked sitting in the chair in the closet. Every room in the house has a small bathroom connected with a shower and toilet and a sink inside. A 55-in TV was hung up on the wall with a queen size bed on the other wall.

"I'm good. I see you feeling yourself." I told her and she smirked.

"Yeah, I'm sipping. I'm trying to figure out why Jamar think he's going out without us." She said and I laughed.

"Me too! It's more fun when y'all come anyways." I told her straight up and she laughed.

"Period, big bro." Karter said and I fired up the blunt taking it to the head.

"What's up sis?" I asked and she smiled. Karter took her drink to her lips and gulped it down.

"Where y'all going?" She asked me and I laughed.

"I knew you wanted something. We going to a club called Sensation." I told her and she nodded.

"Okay, well have fun. Find me a brother-in-law." She said which made me laugh.

"Hold up?" I stopped her because I didn't know that she knew I was gay. I mean, nobody knew I liked men other than Mace. I knew he wasn't gone tell so how the hell did Karter know?

"Boy, I been knowing when you came to dinner at my house a while back actually. You was switching hard as hell then you and C been combined at the hip. I see how you look at him." She said and I nodded.

"I see how he look at you too." She said and I smirked. I

wasn't on that with C. I mean, he was handsome but I wouldn't do him like that. Plus, he was too close to home and I wasn't ready for a relationship.

"Yeah. You know I peep game. Don't tell Jamar I'm popping up either." She said and walked out of the room, leaving me to my thoughts.

After finishing my blunt, I fixed me a shot to get motivated so I could get dressed. I stood in the mirror buttoning up my plaid Burberry shirt. I left the top two buttons undone. I was rocking some Balmain jeans with zippers, and I sprayed my Burberry cologne on. On my feet was some all red Louis Vuitton sneakers. I grabbed my chains and looked at the clock; it was literally 10:18 when I walked out of my room and Charles was coming out of his room at the same time. When we got downstairs, the guys was getting into the truck.

"Pass the bottle up there." I heard Little say and passed one of the Remy Martin bottles to us. We all talked and drank as we made it to the club. When we pulled up to club Sensation it was a whole different scenery. The driver opened the door for us and Charles and I got out first. When we walked through the club females was grabbing all on us; they probably thought we were some type of rappers because the females was flocking to us.

"It's fat in this bitch!" Mace yelled over the music as he wrapped his arms around me. I shook up with him and we went to our section. I ordered me two drinks as the bottle girls started to come to our section.

"I have a few entertainers that wants to come keep you company." A bottle girl said and Jamar nodded then tipped the girls. I sat next to Mace and Charles came and sat by me.

"You good?" I asked and he nodded.

"Yeah I'm chillin. You good?" He asked me and I nodded.

"I'm about to get fucked up." I told him and he laughed.

"I figured; you been drinking since we touched down." Charles said and fired up a blunt.

After a while, the strippers started to come up to our section one by one. It seemed like they smelled that I was gay because the first female that entered our section came straight to me. I waved my hand indicating that I was coo but she started dancing anyway. I wasn't paying her any attention but shorty was bad as hell. The lights in the section went low and Charles leaned over to me.

"She turning you on?" He asked and I shook my head no. I mean, she was bad and if I was straight my dick probably would've been hard but nothing about a female turned me on. I wasn't attracted to women. I loved men.

"Nah, I'm not attracted to women." I told him straight up and he looked at me. He kind of scooted away from me and I laughed. I wasn't trying to make him uncomfortable at all. I was just being honest. I wasn't trying to push up on him or anything but I did find Charles attractive. I wouldn't even fuck with him on that level though; It's not him it's me. I know his past and know how he been hurt. I wouldn't add on to that because I know what I wanted and being in a relationship or even serious with somebody wasn't what I wanted. Not right now anyway.

"You good?" I asked and he shrugged.

"I ain't know. You know, that you were gay." He said and I laughed.

"Nobody knew except Karter and Mace." I told him.

"I ain't think it was anybody business and if anybody wanted to know they would've asked." I added then shrugged. Charles scooted back to his seat and raised his hand to shake up with me. That was his way of showing me he accepted me I guess.

20

KARTER

Stepping into my black thigh high boots I zipped each one up. My black dress hugged my body tightly. I kind of felt a little self-conscious because I still had a very small gut from the baby. I stood in the mirror and examined my butt making sure the dress wasn't too short and my ass wasn't hanging. I must say baby Jamar did get me right. I mean, my ass wasn't little before I had him but now it was just right.

"You look so pretty mommy." Ashtyn said recording me as I fixed my hair in the mirror.

I made sure my jewelry was on and make up was beat. I grabbed my black Chanel purse and kissed Ashtyn on the forehead then kissed Baby Jamar on his little fingers. The rest of the kids was asleep on the floor, while Ashtyn was up in my bed. Jamar and I was sleeping in separate rooms so I ain't mind my kids sleeping with me. Before we left, I made a few phone calls letting the club know I wanted a section right across from my "husband."

"Jamar gonna be pissed when he see us." I said taking a shot with Kris and Bria.

"Yes he is." Lilly agreed and laughed and I rolled my eyes. She was annoying, and I don't know why everybody was so blinded. The bitch was an opp!

"He already said he doesn't want the women to know which club he was going to be at. How did you find out anyways?" Lily asked me which made me roll my eyes.

I ignored her and turned my attention to Kris who was snapping pictures of herself. I didn't fuck with Lily at all. Not because her and Jania was getting close, but because the bitch was just weird! She was the enemy, and once the enemy always the enemy period. I made sure I kept that bitch at a distance because I ain't trust her ass, and I'll always go with my gut. Everybody thought otherwise though, thinking I was jealous but I could care less about all that. Yeah, she was pretty but she wasn't gang, and she shouldn't hang with us. We were putting our self and our family at risk by having this bitch around, I don't care what nobody says. It's gonna come a time when I have to body her ass, and I'mma make sure I empty the clip in this bitch.

"How did you know where they would be at?" Kris asked and I smirked.

"Now you know *MY* husband wasn't leaving the house without me knowing his whereabouts." I said.

"Okay, I know that's right. If you ain't have the pin, trust and believe I did. Mace and I have each other locations on our phones!" Bria said and we slapped hands.

"As y'all should! I always know where my man is at!" Lily said trying to start conversation with us. "Well he isn't my man but he my man." She said and laughed.

"Can't relate!" I shot back and took another shot.

I had to be under the influence to deal with this bitch, and I gotta make sure Jamar knew to stay far away from this hoe. She'll probably try to fuck my nigga with how obsessed she is to make conversation with me.

When we pulled up to the club, it was bangin! The line was wrapped around the building and when we stepped out of the truck the crowd split like the Red Sea.

"Hello, are you Karter?" A lady with a headphone set asked.

"Yes I am." I told her and she smiled.

"Right this way. I have been waiting on you so I can show you your section." She said and held her hand out for us to follow her.

The music was banging and the atmosphere was positive. I grabbed Kris hand as we danced through the crowd.

"Your section is right here." She spoke in my ear and I nodded. I looked across the club to Jamar section and he had a few strippers in there entertaining them so they ain't even notice us. Once we sat down I called the bottle girl over.

"Can you send three bottles of Ace to that section over there." I told her and she nodded. I gave her the money and she walked off. I poured me a drink of whatever they already had in the section and sipped on it. Not long had passed when Jamar stood up and we made eye contact. I stood up and walked to the rails of the section and he laughed. He said something to the dudes and they all looked towards us.

"Let's go dance." I said and everybody jumped up ready to party.

"It's packed as fuck in here." Jania said over the music and I nodded. When I looked back, Lily eyes were on me so I mugged her. The DJ played some slow music as we had fun and danced around the club.

"Damn shorty, what's yo name?" I heard in my ear and I

laughed when I turned around and Jamar was pulling me close to him.

"Karter, what's yo name?" I said playing along with his shenanigans. He pulled me closer and wrapped his arms around my waist as I slow danced on him.

"I'm Jamar but you can call me daddy. You got a man? Fuck all that. I'mma take you from yo nigga." Jamar said which made me bust out laughing.

"I'm single anyways. You don't gotta take me from nobody. Where yo girl at?" I asked and he kissed my neck, sending chills down my body. It's been months since I felt any love and affection. Shit, any type of touch made me horny and ready to go.

"She around here somewhere but I'm worried about you." He said and we both laughed.

"Nigga whatever." I said as he held me tighter.

"You look gorgeous shorty." Jamar whispered in my ear making me blush. I'm not gonna lie, I missed Jamar ass like crazy! I just hope this trip put us in a headspace that we both NEED.

"Thank you Jamar." I said. We danced and after another song he invited us to his section.

"Excuse me... excuse me, this is Karter. These her home girls." Jamar said and everybody looked at him like he was crazy but I laughed.

"We gotta start all over. I'mma make you fall in love with me again." He whispered in my ear once I sat down.

"I never fell out of love Jamar. You still have my heart." I told him honestly and he smiled. He leaned in to kiss me and for a second I hesitated. When our lips touched each other I don't know if he felt what I felt but the butterflies came rushing back. Just by that one simple kiss, Jamar welled me into him like before.

THE NEXT DAY, I rolled over with a slight throbbing in between my legs. I was completely naked and laying in Jamar bed. Jamar was knocked out, mouth wide open, slobber dripping with his arm wrapped around my waist. He was sleeping so peacefully, I didn't want to move. I heard slight snoring and looked at the floor and at the end of the bed, the kids were laying on the covers knocked out.

I snuggled against Jamar chest and closed my eyes. All the flashbacks from last night came rushing back, and my body got hot all over. Jamar sexed my body so good I gotta get a plan b when we go out tonight.

"Good morning." Jamar spoke and I smiled.

"Good morning, Jamar." I responded back and he kissed my forehead.

He stood up and grabbed his shorts off the floor along with a t-shirt, he tossed me a robe and walked out the room. I went to the bathroom connected to his room and handled my hygiene. I slipped my robe on and climbed back into Jamar bed. It was only 8:30 a.m., and I knew we had just went to sleep at five. Jamar came in the room carrying baby Jamar and handed me a bottle, diapers and wipes. He climbed back in the bed under me as I changed and wiped Baby J off.

"I already moved yo stuff in here, so ain't no need for you to go back down there to yo room." Jamar spoke and handed me the bottle so I could feed Baby Jamar. I laughed at his comment and looked at him.

"How you know that I wanna move in here with you?" I asked.

"Girl, when you gave me the pussy, that sealed the deal last night." He smirked and kissed my cheek.

"Yeah okay." I said then handed baby Jamar to him so he could finish feeding him. I laid back on the bed and watched him as he handled the baby.

I couldn't go back to sleep, because a little bit after, the kids started waking up getting in bed with us.

"Good morning mom, dad." Mariel said and snuggled up against Jamar. We had all the kids in the bed with us while they watched TV and Jamar and I talked about anything. This was the best feeling ever.

21

JANIA

"Y'all did what?" I all but yelled as Lily smiled and stood at the sink. We were finally back from Dubai and I hated it. We had so much fun there. I can't wait 'til my birthday. I was making Little take me.

"Yes! I saw him last night at the club, and we had a few drinks. I invited him to my house, and he came. Shit, we didn't even make it to the house because soon as we got in the car I pulled his dick..." Lily said and I smacked my lips.

"Nope, I don't even wanna hear it." I stopped her and finished fixing my dinner. I wasn't up with the shenanigans with Lily and still had my own demons I was fighting. Not trying to be in the middle of nobody else shit.

"Well Jamar, Karter and the kids are coming over for dinner." I told her and her face dropped.

"Together?" She asked and I shook my head. Lily and I grew closer over the past two months or so. She helped me escape but the energy she was giving me lately was different.

"Yes together! What do you expect, Lily? They are married." I told her straight up and she smacked her lips.

"Separated!" She corrected me. Well, tried to because

either way Karter and Jamar was still back together, and Lily was my girl but Karter ain't play about her mans now.

"Bitch, either way that's her husband!" I told her straight up and we heard Jayda's cries from the baby monitor.

"I'll grab her." Lily said and walked away.

I shook my head as I took the last batch of fried chicken out the grease. I was finally getting back to myself. Happy that my appetite was coming back, I made some fried chicken, mashed potatoes, corn on the cob and cornbread. I had the kitchen smelling good and couldn't wait for my friend to get here so I can see how things have been since we have been back.

After taking the cornbread out the oven, the doorbell rang. I saw Lily walk towards the door out of the corner of my eyes and shook my head.

"I got it." She sang and I laughed. She was gone be a problem.

"Hey friendddd." Karter sang as she walked in the kitchen looking like a bad bitch.

Karter always been pretty; she was rocking this short hair style, that I'm guessing Charles did. She had this glow about her and was gorgeous. I loved this Karter; the Karter when her and Jamar was split wasn't the Karter I liked.

"You look bomb Kar." I told her as Jamar and the kids came around the corner. They all was matching each other's fly. Matching Gucci sweaters and Gucci sneakers.

"Thank you babes. You looking good too. Glowing and all." She complimented me and I smiled. Little has been treating me great. I couldn't complain not one bit because he has been by my side and real patient with me.

"Hey y'all." I said and the kids hugged me then ran upstairs to go play. Jamar hugged me and went downstairs to Little's man cave.

"You need any help friend?" Karter asking sitting her purse on the counter and raising up her sleeves.

"No, I'm finished now. Just gotta set the table and bring the food in there." I told her and Lily just stood up in the doorway.

"Hold up, where is Baby Jamar?" I asked and she laughed.

"Yeah, I didn't see him with all the other kids." Lily chimes in and Karter rolled her eyes.

"Why are you talking to me? We are not friends." Karter said and turned her attention back to me.

"But Jania, *FRIEND*, he with C and Mason." She told me and I nodded.

"Okay that's coo." I told her as she helped me take the food to the dining room and set the table. Once the table was set and the kids table was set, we made their plates and set it on their table. Karter went to get Little and Jamar while I went to get the kids.

"SOMEBODY SAY GRACE." I said and Karter stood up.

"I will." She said and we held hands. Lily tried to grab Karter hand but she moved it and I sighed. I hope Karter ain't get on no grade A bullshit.

"Father God thank you for the food we are about to receive. Thank you for bringing my family back together, and we will forever believe in you Father God. Amen." She spoke and my stomach turned upside down. I saw Lily smirking out the corner of my eyes and put my head down. This was about to be a long ass night.

"This food looks good." Little said and I smiled.

"Thanks babe." I thanked him and started to eat.

"Jamar and I are going house shopping soon. We were

thinking Thanksgiving at our house this year." Karter spoke and I nodded.

"That should be fun. I'm down. Just let me know what you want me to bring and you know I'm down." I told her chewing the food in my mouth.

"That's good. Well, I'm going back to my home town soon, but I should be back before Thanksgiving so let me know what you want me to bring also." Lily said and Karter laughed.

"I don't like you, so you won't be invited to my house." Karter spoke and Lily gasped.

"Karter!" Jamar called her name and Karter looked at him.

"I'm being honest." She said and I sighed.

"Okay, I don't care that you don't like me. Everybody else does including your husband." Lily said and Karter stood up.

"Let's go." Jamar cheating ass said and I sat my fork down.

"Kids, go get y'all stuff." I told them and all the kids got up and ran out of the dining room.

Soon as Karter kids got far away, Karter reached over the table and hit Lily dead in the face. Lily recovered fast though and hit Karter back. Karter grabbed Lily by the back of the shirt and started hitting her in the face, meanwhile Lily tried to swing but her hits weren't connecting because every time Karter connected Lily slowed down. Jamar tried to grab Karter and Little grabbed Lily only for Lily to fall backwards and Karter got on top of her beating her ass. I helped Jamar grab Karter but she turned on him and started swinging on him.

"Bitch, you got me so fucked up!" Karter started to say but Jamar held Karter's hands.

"I'mma fuck you up and when I'm done, I'mma fuck yo nigga!" Lily yelled and Karter started to swing on Jamar again. Little pushed Lily towards the door and when he got her outside Jamar let Karter go.

"Did you know about that?" Karter asked me and I stood there.

I couldn't say no because I did, but I wouldn't dare tell my best friend that her husband was fucking on a bitch I brought in the family. My loyalty lied with Karter, and I know how she feels about that loyalty shit.

"You did, didn't you? Wow, you had this bitch around me and she was fucking my husband!" Karter said on the verge of tears. She started to walk towards Jamar and he backed up. I was laughing on the inside because he looked scared as fuck. I mean, I know this big ass nigga wasn't scared of her little bitty ass.

"It's not..."Jamar started to say but Karter picked up a plate off the table and threw it towards him.

"Bitch don't you fucking say it! You was fucking this bitch whole time?" She asked Jamar and he couldn't say shit.

"Take me home before I kill everybody in this bitch!" Karter snapped. She picked her purse up and on her way out she didn't forget to deck my ass in the face which made me see stars for a little bit. Damn, what a fucking night!

22

JAMAR

"You not gone let me explain! I ain't even fuck that bitch. She was saying that to make you mad!" I yelled through the door.

"Bye Jamar! You're trespassing so if you don't leave right now I'mma shoot yo ass!" She yelled then I heard the gun cock back. I hit the door and stepped back. I hopped in the car and Mariel and Jamie was fighting.

"Chill out with that shit man!" I snapped not really meaning to take my anger out on the kids.

I was just pissed that I was caught up in more bullshit with Karter. I mean, really I didn't cheat. I don't know why Lily wanted to bring up the fact that she sucked my dick *ONCE* now. That happened well over three months ago and now she wanted to get messy! I know it's only because Karter and I finally got back together. She was hurt because she was throwing shots that she wanted to fuck with me heavy but I shut that shit down. Since she wanted to be messy, I was definitely gone murk that bitch before it was all said and done.

"Pops, ma is really mad!" KJ said and I sighed.

"Yeah she is, but don't take your anger out on us!" Ashtyn smart ass said as I bit the inside of my jaws.

"Dad, what did you do? Mommy was just so happy now she's sad again." Mariel said so softly and confused, which made me feel more like shit. I was fucking up badly and my kids was starting to see how hurtful I was being too they mother.

"I'm sorry y'all. I'mma fix it." I told them and Ashtyn sighed. She mumbled something under her breath then put her headphones on. I grabbed my phone then ordered some pizza. After I ordered the food, I called Karter; she answered on the last ring.

"What's up, something wrong with the kids?" She asked and I sighed. I knew it was a reason why she answered and that was the kids. Any other time she wouldn't have answered and that's been like that for the past three days.

"Nah, they good. How's my baby?"

Karter hung up the phone, and I threw my phone in the cup holder. Beefing with Kar was straight bullshit!! We just got back good and that was the best feeling I had in a long time. Being with shorty and my seeds I can finally breathe again. Us into it was like a knife stuck in my side. I was sick right now because she wasn't fucking with me. This wasn't a normal fuck-up either. She told me on several different occasions how she ain't fuck with Lily and I still went against the grain and let that filthy whore suck my dick.

Ring Ring Ring.

"Hello?" I answered my mother Eva call. She wasn't fucking with me either. I was really surprised that she was even calling me.

"Bring my grandbabies to me." She said then hung up. It

was my weekend but shit I might as well. They wasn't fucking with me because I hurt their momma. That's wild how loyal they were to their mom. Shit, every time Karter and I got into it they sided with her.

"Y'all grandma want y'all to come over." I told them and they all yelled *yay*.

"Good cause I was gonna have my momma come get me anyways." Ashtyn said and rolled her eyes at me.

I wanted to wring her little ass neck, but I waited to get to my dukes crib so I could talk to her. Ashtyn was grown as hell and getting beside herself. That mouth and attitude, I don't know where she get that from and when it became that smart. It wasn't cute and it was too grown for her little young ass.

Pulling up to the pizza place, I went in and grabbed the pizzas then headed to my duke crib. Charles car was parked out and I groaned. Charles and Kar was close as hell. I know if Charles know I fucked up with Kar again he gone be all in our business.

"Alright, let's go." I told them as I grabbed the pizzas.

Me and my crew went in and walked to the kitchen. After taking my coat off, I washed my hands and got their plates together.

"Sit at the table and eat." I told them as I sat Karson in the high chair and gave him a pizza. I went downstairs to the family room where I heard C and my momma talking. As soon as I hit the bottom step, I felt a hit connect to the side of my face.

"What I told you last time?" Charles said and squared up.

He threw another punch but this time I dodged it. I knew this nigga was gone be beefy but I couldn't believe he wanted all smoke with me over *my wife*. I got in my fighting stance and smiled. I felt like that little thirteen year old boy again getting ready to whoop a nigga ass. I ain't fought in so long so I wanted the first hit. I swung and decked him in the jaw. He recovered fast and swung then popped me in the side. We went blow for blow until he slammed me on the ground and got on top of me. We both were swinging though. I wasn't stopping and neither was he.

I was getting tired so I grabbed Charles and put him in the head lock.

"That's enough." Eva said laughing. I pushed him backwards and he held his hand up to help me. After he helped me up we shook up and hugged.

"I beat yo ass this time." Charles said and we both laughed.

"Yeah, he got you Jamar." Eva said agreeing but I ain't say nothing. I just sat down and sighed.

"Yeah nigga, you sick about this shit! You should be." Charles said and sat next to me.

"She ain't fucking with you, and I don't blame her." Eva said as she took a sip of her cup. I shook my head cause damn! They was on a nigga.

"Want me tell you how to get her back?" Charles asked leaning towards me. I looked at him and hesitated.

"Yeah, come on. Tell me what I gotta do cause she ain't fucking with me." I told Charles and he pulled his phone out. He started talking about ordering, renting and buying shit. This nigga was tryna plan a wedding, doing the most. After an hour of talking, giving me tips, and spending money I went to the crib lonely and by myself.

∼

THE NEXT DAY, I pulled up to the building and waited until

Charles and Karter came out. They were going to look for a new shop for C to buy. This was the third place I followed them to, and I guess they ain't like this one either. Following after them, C did a U-turn and hit the dash going the opposite way. I did also and followed them to Karter house. When we pulled to the gates, the police was sitting trying to get in. I hopped out right after Karter did.

"Excuse me, what's going on here?" She asked pulling her shades over her eyes. "I got a call from my security office telling me that my alarm has been going off for the last thirty minutes." Karter also said which made me clutch on my pistol.

"Yeah, when you didn't answer, Mrs. Taylor, we were notified." One of the policeman said and Karter nodded.

"But when we got here we couldn't get in." He chuckled and Karter smiled.

"Sorry. We got it under control." Karter said then looked back and mugged me. I went back to my car as the police got in theirs. Karter punched her code in the gate, and it started to raise up. I followed her through and hopped out of the car with her and C.

"Go home Jamar." She snapped once she saw me and I ignored her. She stopped at the door and turned to me.

"Was you following us?" she asked annoyed, and I smirked.

"Girl, nobody was following you. I just drove by and saw y'all out here." I lied and she sighed. Charles pulled his piece out and so did I. Karter did the same and we went into her house. We weren't even all the way in and saw it was fucked up just by the door.

"Wowwww." She said and stood shocked.

Reality must've hit because she ran towards the stairs taking two at a time. Charles looked at me and we followed her. When she got to her room she went to the bathroom and moved the rug that was on the floor. She moved a tile over and peeled a box from the floor. Karter opened the box and sighed. She poured the contents on the floor and stacks of money fell.

"Damn shawty. What you hustling?" I asked and she laughed.

"Hell nah, nigga, I save!" She said and looked around. Whoever broke into Karter's crib fucked her shit up.

"Well, I guess it's time to move." She shrugged and went to her room. She started throwing stuff on her bed and putting shit in bags. I shook my head and started helping her.

"Y'all can stay with me until I find us a house." I told Karter.

"Boy boo. My kids can stay with you. I'll stay with C or shit my momma." Karter spoke and looked at me.

"Just tell me this and I'm not gone ask shit else." She said and I ran my hands down my face. *Here she goes.*

"What's up Kar?" I wondered leaning against her dresser.

"When did y'all fuck?" She asked and looked at me.

"We never fucked! She gave me head for literally thirty seconds after one day I had passed out on Little couch. We went out one night after Jania had the baby. I was fucked up. Shorty head was so trash I thought it was a dream. When I realized it wasn't I pushed her off. We never fucked. She don't got my number. She probably can't even tell you what my dick look like." I told Karter straight up and she sighed.

"You should've told me though! That bitch shouldn't have thought she had one up on me!" Karter yelled and I nodded. I knew she was hurt, but I wish she knew how much I loved her and wouldn't dare disrespect her like that.

She was my wife, my heart! I put her little ass through too much already, and I wouldn't dare do her like that again.

"Karter, you know I love you. You the only woman I ever gave my heart. I married you. I wouldn't do you like that shorty." I told her honestly and she shrugged.

"It is what it is." She stood up and walked out of her room. "I'm about to check the cameras." She yelled over her shoulders and I followed her.

When Charles walked in we were already sitting at the desk cutting the computers on. I leaned on the wall behind Karter as she fooled around with her computer. Footage of the house popped up and Karter fast forwarded. Charles leaned on the desk and tapped his finger as we waited until somebody came in view. A figure walked into the house and shut the door. When she turned around, Karter gasped.

"This bitch!" she stood and snapped. I looked closer and saw Lily walk through Karter house tearing up everything. Karter paced back and forth while I watched shorty fuck up the whole entire house.

"I'mma kill that hoe!" Karter snapped and I shut the computers down. I didn't even say nothing because I knew Lily was on that fuck shit because she wanted me.

"I wonder if she found what she was looking for." Charles said and Karter sighed.

"I'm ready." she said and walked out the room. I followed after her. I knew she was defeated and didn't have any fight left in her. I just got in my car and left. She wasn't fucking with me, and I know she ain't wanna be bothered with me.

23

LILY

Well since this is my first and last chapter I might as will give it to ya raw and uncut. Fuck that bitch Karter and fuck Jania too if she was riding with Karter. Yeah, I broke into the bitch house because I wanted her to know it was smoke! She tried to sneak me at dinner but next time it won't happen again. I'mma make sure she regret ever putting her hands on me.

I wasn't even gone fuck with Jamar like that but she kept coming for me. Guaranteed I topped Jamar off before I told Jania and I lied a little bit too but so what! I didn't fuck with that bitch, and I knew she was sick when she found out I had her nigga wide open.

Smack, Smack, Smack!

"Du yu hea wut mi sayn?" My uncle Marley snapped in his broken English.

He smacked the table breaking me out of my daydream. I quickly nodded and tried to pay attention. If it wasn't about getting little miss Karter out the way then I wasn't with it. She was in the way for real. I know after she find out

I´m the one that broke into her house she was gone be pissed.

"Did you forget why you went there in the first place. It seem like you forgot the goal!" Vanessa burnt up ass said. I looked at her face and laughed.

"Bitch, I don't work for you so stop talking to me." I told her as she rolled her eyes.

"Get us an address tomorrow." Vanessa ordered and walked away. She had a few people following after her and once they were gone it was just me and my uncle by ourselves.

"I'm not helping you kill Jamar." I told him firmly and he laughed in my face. I sighed because I know what I was about to say was either gone go one way or the other. I was ready for whatever though.

"Yu dink he luh yu? He tuk Yu fahda." My uncle said which made me roll my eyes.

"Yeah after y'all took his people! Look, I'm not helping you get Jamar! That's that." I told Marley and he looked at me.

"He's gonna die. Whoever stand in du way will get it tu!" he told me and I laughed in his face. I hope he wasn't threatening me at all. Marley know I will handle him without a problem, and I wasn't letting him or nobody else stop me from being with Jamar.

"You like him?" Marley asked reading me like a book. He was right though. I didn't just like him; I loved Jamar. The way he smelled, talked, the way he was a boss. He had me wide open from the very first time I saw him.

I wanted him badly and after I took out Karter I was gone make it my business to have him.

"Look, I'm nat gunna let yu stand in de way! Jamar and his whole family are gonna die." Marley said and I stood up.

I grabbed the gun I kept on my side and before he could even see what was going on I had already fired two shots killing him.

"And I'mma kill anybody that think they're gonna stand in my way of being with him." I said and grabbed my purse and left out the same way I came in.

The whole way home I had no remorse on what I just did. Really, that just made the job easier for Jamar. I had no family left, because Jamar done got rid of everybody. Vanessa was the only person my uncle had and after I told Jamar her hiding spot he wouldn't hesitate to go handle her.

That's how I'mma win him back by giving him Vanessa and Marley's address and when he goes to that spot, he gone see Marley already dead then handle V. I'mma handle Karter, marry Jamar, be the perfect step-mother, and have his kids.

When I pulled up at the crib, I shut my car off and went inside. I grabbed my house phone, went to the back room and dialed Jamar's cell phone.

"Hello?" He answered and I blushed. His voice was so soothing and welcoming. I just wanted to hear him talk.

"Soon we'll be together baby." I told him and the line went dead. His phone must've lost service. I sat in the middle of the floor with my legs crossed. The pictures of Jamar plastered around the room made me tingle inside. I bowed my head and started to pray.

"You really are fucking crazy!" I heard behind me and laughed.

"I knew you'd be showing up once you figured out it was me who destroyed your house." I told Karter.

"It's funny because I kept telling everyone you wasn't supposed to be here, but hey, nobody listens to me." She told me.

"If it wasn't for me, Jania wouldn't be here and it's fuck her if she riding with you. I'mma kill your lil sexy ass then fuck your husband and give him more kids while raising the ones you birthed for him." I told her.

"Ew, the fact that you're even attracted to something that's already taken is sick. I wanted to come here and beat your ass but you ain't even worth my energy." She said as she shot me in the knee and I dropped.

"You just feel threatened knowing I'mma take your spot." I tried to spit at her.

"Only spot you taking up is the one in hell bitch!" She said and shot me right between the eyes.

24

EVA

"God, please just send my baby home so I can have a proper burial." I begged as I moved around the kitchen.

I woke up in my feelings. Usually, when I cooked on Thanksgiving I had Tiera here with me. Today was going on ten months and I haven't heard her voice. Guarantee she was out here moving foul, but that was still my daughter and I missed her. Even if she wasn't alive, I wanted her body so we could bury her properly. My tears were all dried out. I prayed daily for my kids, and this hit home when Tiera didn't come home.

Knock, knock, knock!

"Who is it?" I asked wiping my hands on a napkin walking towards the door.

I peeked through the glass and it was Karter, Jamar, and the kids. Seeing them put a smile on my face so I put Tiera in the back of my mind.

"Hey ma." Karter spoke then kissed my cheek.

She had the baby in her arms while Jamar carried bags. I

kissed each one of my grandbabies as they walked through the house.

After Jamar put the bags in the kitchen, Karter gave the baby to him while she helped me in the kitchen.

"How has your morning been?" Karter asked me.

I smiled and thought back on the first time Jamar brought her home to meet me. I was just so happy that somebody came in and got Jamar's mind off the streets. Karter definitely came in and stole his heart. I was glad because she blessed me with those pretty grandbabies.

"I been cool. I see you glowing or whatever." I complimented her because she was glowing.

"I mean this that 'fuck nigga' free glow." She joked and laughed. I didn't blame her though. These girls went through the most with loving their men. I mean, I wish I had that type of strength to stay with a man. With me, it's one fuck-up then yo ass was kicked to the curb. I guess that was my toxic trait.

"Girl whatever!" I said back as we finished cooking.

After a few hours of slaving over the stove, and family coming, the food was finally done and everybody had showed up.

"Okay you guys, thank you all for coming. I'm glad we all could come together and enjoy each other's company." Janet spoke and I smiled. I stood next to her and put my arm around her shoulders.

"Thank you to Karter and Jamar for bringing all you wonderful people into my life. At first, I was worried about Jamar being with Kar because he was so advanced for his age and so much older acting than her. Y'all both balance each other out though. You accepted my grandboy with open arms so for that I thank you for coming to my family and being a blessing to us." Janet said and I hugged her.

"Well, I wanna say thank the Lord for bringing us all back together! I'mma thank the Lord every day for that. I also wanna thank the Lord, because like my sis Janet said, he brought some wonderful people into my life." I said and sat down. Every Thanksgiving we went around and told what we were thankful for. I was ready to eat so I made it short for me.

"Okay, I just wanna say thank you to my mother for raising a bomb ass bitch!" Kris joked and we all laughed. "No but for real, I guess I wanna say thank you, Mommy, because without you I wouldn't be here. And thank you to the most high for putting my husband Brandon in my life." She said and Brandon started to smile.

When Kris sat down he pecked her on the lips. It was his turn but he said he wanted to go last so we went to the next person which was Little. Little said a few words and then it was Jania turn. She coughed then stood up.

"Okay, I just wanna say this, and I know it's not the place but Karter I'm sorry. I didn't know that Lily liked Jamar. Right before you had got there she told me. I was gone tell you but..." Jania rambled off but Karter stood up. She walked around the table to Jania then Little stood up. I was praying that Karter ain't hit the girl again.

"No need to explain. Shorty is handled and I forgive you bestie." Karter said and they hugged. I could tell Karter was still bothered but she was being the bigger person. Besides she couldn't be mad at Jania when she clearly forgave Jamar.

"I just want to say I'm thankful for you all accepting me like I was one of y'all own. Momma E, you accept my kids as your grandchildren and love them unconditionally. I will always have love for every one of you guys and respect y'all. So thanks everyone." Jania spoke and sat down. Little passed and it was Karter turn. She stood up and pulled a paper out of her pocket. *Here she goes.*

"Okay, first I'm just thankful for the most high for bringing me to this point in my life, humbling me, breaking me down and building me back up. I also want to thank my dukes because she made me the strong woman I am today. I made it in life because my mother pushed me not to give up. So thank you, Mom. I'm also very thankful for Jamar sadly." she said then smiled. "Jamar, you turned me into a woman and although I thought I was grown when I had Kartier, being your wife turned me into a woman. Your love and loyalty showed me how to be a woman. I'm forever grateful and thankful for you, Jamar. You blessed me with three beautiful children biologically but you have shared six kids with me. I'm forever thankful for them six reasons alone. So my biggest thank you is to you Jamar." Karter said then sat down.

She had a single tear in her eye and wiped it. Jamar stood up and smirked.

"I didn't write anything down but all my thanks go to the most high of course. He brought every last one of my loved one into my heart. So he gets all my thanks." Jamar said and I nodded. Brandon stood up and pulled a paper out his pockets.

"It's taking me a lot to say this so bear with me." Brandon said then awkwardly laughed.

"Some of you don't know but the day Charles got kidnapped my wife and I admitted myself into a rehabilitation center. In that center I was taught how to grieve properly, forgive and forget and to love myself and my friends. I'm thankful because I made it out of that situation and couldn't be happier. I'm thankful because although Kris divorced me she never left my side the whole time, so Kris." Brandon got down on one knee and everybody gasped.

I was shocked as hell about everything he had just said so I just stood there watching with my mouth ajar.

"Kris I would love to raise your child as mine. So if you would like to will you marry me again?" Brandon said then pulled a ring box out his pocket. Kris jumped up and down and hugged him. She kept saying yes over and over again and after a while I just sat down and started to eat. I was hungry shit!

25

LITTLE

"So listen, when we go in there just leave Mister alive." Jamar said and I nodded.

It felt good having the whole crew back. I mean when C got kidnapped, Brandon went to rehab so Jamar and myself was out here in the streets by ourselves. The crew was broken when it was Jamar and me. Now that Charles and B was back we were complete and back focused.

"Man, look at this shit! Who the hell is that?" Brandon asked, and we sat back and looked at the car. Vanessa got out the car and we all smiled. I guess this was our time to shine.

"Kill two birds with one gun. Don't let them escape this time. They had too many chances." Jamar spoke and when we were about to get out Vanessa came back out and was talking on the phone. I was glad we were ducked off in a spot where nobody could see us because she pulled out the driveway and parked on the curb.

"What this bitch on?" Charles said, and I leaned back looking at the house then to Vanessa.

"Let's just murk this bitch!" Jamar said and I put my hand up.

"Just wait and see what she on." I said and we sat back.

After a while, police, ambulance, and fire trucks pulled up. They went inside then Vanessa pulled off. Brandon pulled off following her.

"That nigga might be in there dead." Jamar said and that made logical sense. Vanessa was in and out and then why would she wait for the police and ambulance to get there to leave. I was confused about the whole little play out.

"Just keep up and see where she going!" Charles said, I'm guessing getting agitated.

Vanessa made a sharp left then Brandon did the same. She started to drive faster winging in and out of traffic but Bran stayed on her ass.

"She know we on her ass, so when I speed up bust the tires!" Brandon said, and Charles cocked his pistol back and got in position.

Soon as Vanessa hit the left, Charles took the back tires out making her car swerve. She hit another left going into a dead end, Charles hopped out of the car and ran to the car. He fired three shots and then came back to the car. He nodded and we got the fuck out of dodge.

∽

"I'M JUST glad you doing everything to get yourself back right." I told Jania and she smiled.

After all this time being back home, Jania and I could finally go out without being watched, or being cautious that somebody was aiming for us. I was glad my wife was finally back to herself also.

"Thank you for being patient with me. I'm so happy we

are back like we used to be." She told me and picked up the menu. After we both looked over the menu, I waved for the waitress to come. Jania ordered first then I did.

"Do you know what you wanna do for Ty birthday?" I asked Jania and she shrugged.

"It's really up to him. He said he wanted to go to Disney World, and I think that'll be a fun family vacation for the kids." Jania responded then took a sip of her drink. "We going to get the kids today. I want to end the night with our kids." Jania said, and I smiled.

Jania and I was just now finally getting back on track and I was loving it. She had me feeling like when we first started talking. I loved this feeling, and even though I never fell out of love with her, she made me fall more in love with her. If that makes sense.

"You look sexy as fuck shorty." I told her and she smirked.

Jania's make-up was flawless, and Charles had just did her some style with long weave. My shorty was gorgeous.

"You keep looking at me like this, we gone have to say fuck dem kids and go straight home." She joked and we laughed. I was on whatever she was on though, so after dinner, we went straight home.

THE NEXT DAY, I woke up to an empty bed. I searched for my phone and replied to missed messages and emails as I went to the bathroom to handle my hygiene.

Walking downstairs, I could hear Jania laughing with Karter, Kris, and Bria.

"God forgive me but I'mma kill any bitch that Jamar ever fuck with! The little bitch Jessie got murked soon as I came home from the hospital. I didn't even wait a full six weeks until I sprained in action!" I heard Karter say and shook my head. I rounded the corner and cleared my throat.

"You sis and all, but don't be giving my girl no ideas, please!" I told Karter.

"Shid, if anything we got our ideas from each other if you catch my drift." Karter said winking at me.

"Yeah, I know all too well, and that's the scary part." I replied knowing Karter was talking bout the Tiera situation.

Speaking of that, I'm going to go holler at Jamar about it cause it's about that time to get it off my chest. Once I showered and handled my hygiene, I headed out to go speak with my mans.

26

JAMAR

"Hello?" I answered my ringing phone.

"Wassup my dude, what's the word?" Little asked me.

"Not shit man. Think I'm bout to have Karter meet a nigga for lunch. I'm hungry thenna bitch." I told him as my stomach growled.

"Shoot me the restaurant. Me and my shorty will meet y'all there." Little told me hanging up.

I got up to shower and handle all my hygiene needs in peace since the kids were over at my mom's crib for the weekend. Once I was dried off, I pulled on my Ethika draws and threw on a red Ralph Lauren jogging suit with the new, *What The* retro Jordan four's, that just dropped. I squirted a couple squirts of my Polo Red cologne that Karter had got me which was becoming my favorite smell.

I was feeling good so I decided to bring out the Hummer that was painted candy red sitting on foes! We decided on Benihana's for lunch; I could use some hanichi. Little and Jania was going to meet me and Karter there. Karter was first to arrive of course, and when I spotted her, I approached her noticing the glow she had to her.

I wasn't surprised when she told me Lily wasn't a problem for us. Karter showed me a different side of her every day. I was just glad we were past that and could finally get back to how we used to be.

"Hey honey." Karter greeted then hugged me. She kissed my cheeks, and I pulled out her chair to sit. I sat next to her.

"You glowing. How has yo day been?" I asked her and she weakly smiled.

"I'm good. I been feeling so damn tired lately." She told me.

"You know, you got that glow to you like I popped another seed in you." I told her smirking.

"Ununt no sir, I would know if I was pregnant Jock." she replied but I could tell she was in deep thought.

"Well, how about after this we go get a test." I suggested.

"We can if that'll make you feel better hubby." She told me and kissed my lips.

We ordered lemonades while we waited on Little and Jania. Ten minutes later, they came walking in and my nigga looked nervous as hell. It's bout to be some shit.

"Wassup my nigga, wassup sis." I said hugging Jania and shaking up with Little. The waitress came back, and I went ahead and ordered. I was starving.

"I'll take the chicken and steak hibachi, with the chicken fried rice." I told the waiter and waited til everyone else ordered. I was eager to know what Little was on edge about.

"We thinking about Disney World for Ty birthday this year." Jania announced breaking the tension that was building.

"That sounds fun. Let me know the dates and things and we can get it together." Karter said.

"I'm tired of holding this secret in!" Little blurted out. Now I was even more interested as I leaned back and sipped my drink.

"What secret?" I asked curiously.

"Tell him babe." Little nudged Jania and said.

"Um, I killed Tiera." Jania said low as hell whispering and shit.

"You know I can't hear you. Speak up." I told her.

"Tiera followed me one day and forced herself into my house with a gun. She told me she was gone kill me and some other shit. I told her I wasn't ready to die over no nigga; she could have him. I told her about Charles missing and she let her guard down and I tackled her. We wrestled for the gun a bit and that's when the shit went off. I shot her once and once I realized what I had done I tried to check on the baby..." Jania rambled off.

"You tried to check on the baby and?" I asked.

"It wasn't no fucking baby Jamar. This bitch was faking all along. She had a muthafucking fake ass stomach on!" Jania raised her voice and I sighed.

I didn't know what to say. I know Tiera was moving funny, and I can't say I didn't miss my sister. I missed the her before Little.

"Y'all gotta tell mama cause I won't be the one to break the news to her." I said after sitting in my thoughts.

"Really Jamar? I barely had the guts to tell you let alone mama." Jania said.

"Well one of y'all is going to tell her but it won't be me. After lunch, we all gone go together." I said ending the conversation. For the remainder of the lunch, it was awkward because Karter tried to keep the conversation between us but was failing miserably.

Arriving to dukes' crib, I hopped out first to go make

sure my mama was ready for what she was about to hear. She was in the kitchen cooking with her music on. I damn near felt bad for what's about to happen.

"Hey baby. I was just about to call you guys and tell y'all to come over." She said and hugged me then Karter.

We sat down at the island in the middle of the kitchen as Little and Jania walked in. Jania was looking sad and I sighed. I didn't care about her feelings though. This shit was about to break my dukes' heart for real.

"What's wrong with y'all?" My momma Eva asked and cut the radio down.

"The day Charles got kidnapped, I had went home because I thought I left the stove on. Tiera forced herself in my house with a gun and basically told me that since I wouldn't leave Little alone she was gonna kill me." Jania paused for a second and my momma sat down. I could see the wheels in her head turning. So I stood up to comfort her.

"We fought for the gun and it went off. I tried to save her but she died instantly. She was never pregnant, ma. Teira was wearing a fake stomach this whole time. I didn't know what else to do. I was so scared." Jania said and my momma sighed deeply.

"GET OUT! GET THE FUCK OUT MY HOUSE RIGHT NOW!" My dukes told Jania and she looked at me. I nodded to both of them, and they turned and walked away.

"Jamar, did you know?" She asked me.

I could tell she was hurt by that but I didn't have no emotions. Sadly, Tiera was my sis but she made her bed when she turned to the other side.

"No. I wish I could have put a bullet in her instead." I told my mother truthfully, and she looked at me.

"Ma, I told you she was working with the other side! She

was ready to give ALL of us up because she couldn't fucking have that man!" I snapped, and my mother didn't say nothing.

"She put my kids in danger and even her own kids in danger as well because she was a scorned woman! FUCK THAT!" I snapped and sat back by Karter.

"GET THE FUCK OUT JAMAR! GET YO BLACK ASS OUT MY HOUSE!" She screamed getting into my face.

I tried to hug her but she pushed me away. I don't know why I thought my dukes was gone see my side. I won't say I didn't miss my sister. I think about her ass every day, but she let dick cloud her judgement and switched up. For that, she paid the price.

"JUST GO!" My momma screamed but I wasn't letting up. I grabbed her wrist and pulled her to me and she hugged me. She wasn't crying, but I know her heart was hurting right now. Karter hugged her, too, and we stood in the kitchen comforting one another.

∽

"WE GOOD?" Little asked walking over to me.

I nodded and we shook hands. He hugged me tightly, and I could tell he was relieved. Jania walked over to me with Karter and we hugged.

"We gone put this chapter behind us. Everybody in this room is family." Little spoke and I agreed.

"Okay babe, I have to run. Are you good with the kids?" Karter asked and I nodded.

"I'll be back after my appointment." She said then kissed my lips. Karter hurried off and waved for Jania. Jania and Karter left leaving me and my boy Little with the kids.

"Ma dukes called me yesterday." Little said and I nodded.

I knew my mother was fucked up about the shit with Tiera, but I know my momma cause I was just like her. She didn't play about that loyalty and once I gave her the facts about Tiera working with Vanessa nem, my momma was hurt! She'll get over it though; it was either our whole entire family or her. I'm sorry, baby sis; it had to be you. Just didn't think Jania would be the one to take her.

"What she say?" I asked, and he sat down next to where I was sitting.

"She said she forgave Jania and don't hold no hard feelings. She had to think and if it was her she would've done the same thing. She also said she was just mad because we kept it from her." Little told me and I nodded. I was just happy that everything was behind us. It seemed like we had more problems every day. I was ready to enjoy life and relax.

"What's up with you? I mean, I know shit been rocky, but you really about to let sis do that shit?" He asked me which caught me off guard.

"What do you mean? Do what?" I asked silently praying he wasn't about to tell me Karter was about to do something real fucking stupid..

"Aw shit bro. Wifey said Kar about to go to the chop shop."

SEVEN - KARTER

I was nervous as hell when I pulled up to the abortion clinic. First of all, it seemed like this bitch Jania was wasting time. My appointment was at three, and this bitch took the longest way here. Now she was taking forever to park.

"Bitch, you annoying!" I snapped getting out my car slamming the door shut. She pissed me off and as much as I said I forgave her about the Lily shit I still wasn't fucking with her like that!

"GOD IS WATCHING YOU!" I heard from behind me, and it was a group of people protesting which made my stomach drop.

"Just give me the baby! It'll be my first." Another protester yelled, and I kept walking. As soon as I got to the door, I pulled it open but it was slammed shut making the glass doors crack.

"Have you lost yo motherfucking mind?" Jamar shouted as he got in my face. I could've sworn I saw horns sticking up from his head. I didn't even speak, because Jamar was so mad, I saw the smoke coming from his ears.

"I'MMA COUNT TO THREE, KARTER, AND IF YOU NOT IN THE CAR BY THEN I'MMA BREAK YO NECK!" Jamar said sternly and forcefully.

I nodded and walked to his car without even saying bye to Jania. Jamar stood at the door of the clinic and then turned to come to his car. I waved to Jania and she smiled waving bye. I knew that bitch gave me up! She ain't want me to get an abortion in the first place. *Fuck.*

The whole way to Jamar's house, he didn't say one word to me. I didn't care, though, because as much as he was mad, I was mad also! Shit, we already had a full house. How could he blame me! We didn't need any more kids running around.

"You tripping shorty for real." Jamar snapped as he unlocked the door and walked in. I didn't reply back. I just kicked my shoes off and went up the stairs calling Charles.

"Hello?" He answered on the first ring, and I sighed feeling the tears come to my eyes.

"I'm so annoyed right now." I said as I tried to hold the tears.

This baby had me emotional as hell, and Jamar didn't understand the cause of being pregnant. I did this shit four fucking times. My body was tired of having fucking babies. I'm only twenty-six years old, and I have five kids. I'm tired of fucking kids! I been having kids since I was a damn kid. Can I catch a fucking break? I feel like Jamar was being real selfish getting me pregnant anyway!

"What's wrong sus?" Cici asked.

"I tried to go get my abortion and Jamar popped up. That dumb ass bitch Jania told on me. I can't wait to beat that bitch ass!" I yelled getting infuriated again.

"I'm getting real sick and tired of this hoe." Ci said, and I sighed because I was too. The fact that this bitch told Jamar that I was getting an abortion made me even more mad. I know time was gone come when I have to tag that bitch, AGAIN!

"I am too! It's like Jamar don't even give a fuck. I love my kids dearly, but I'm so tired of being pregnant! It seem like I'm having a baby every fucking year. I'm ready to live life, start a business and do what I wanna do!" I vented and Jamar came in the room with a mean mug on his face. I tried to get up and walk out but he grabbed my arm pulling me back.

"Get off the phone! Let me holla at you!" he said and let my arm go. I sighed and told Charles I would call him back later. I sat on the foot stool in the middle of our room. I kept sneaking glances at Jamar but I couldn't really look into his eyes.

"Look at me!" He snapped and I looked up. Soon as our eyes connected, the tears started falling.

"Don't cry now. What you crying for?" He asked me and I sighed. Soon as I was about to talk Jamar stood up and paced the floor. "You was really about to kill my seed Karter?" He asked hurt dripping from his voice.

"I mean, I know we have been through some shit, and I ain't been the best husband but damn shorty." He said and looked at me.

"Jamar, you wouldn't understand that I'm sick of being pregnant. We have six kids, Jamar, SIX! When you get mad and you leave and be gone for days it's me that's here still taking care of them. I get up every morning to cook breakfast for them, homework, cleaning, everything involving them six kids IT'S ME! I carry them for ten months and take the risk. I'm tired Jamar!" I told him truthfully and he stood up.

"Do what you wanna do shorty!" He said and walked out

of the room slamming the door making the family picture of us fall to the ground breaking.

∼

"Mommy." Mariel screamed as I walked into Jania and Little's house. The kids stayed a night over here last night.

"You don't see yo uncle here?" Charles said and put his hand on his hips.

"Uncle C!" Ashtyn said as she ran down the steps. We were still standing in the foyer waiting on all the kids to come down.

"Pops is down there. He came and stayed the night with us last night. We were up playing games all night." Kartier said hugging my legs.

"Okay, go get y'all coats!" I told them and they ran off. After all the kids got their coats and stuff on, Jania came down the stairs carrying Baby Jamar. I couldn't help but to roll my eyes.

"Take my baby." I told Charles, and he already knew what was about to happen so he gathered the baby stuff and ushered the kids out of the house.

"Kar, please don't be mad at me. I was just...."

I didn't even let her finish her sentence before I cocked back and punched her dead in the mouth.

"Stay the fuck out my business, bro. Fuck you, and I'm coo off yo fraud ass!" I snapped and she rushed me tackling me to the ground.

Jania got on top of me but that didn't stop me from throwing punches. She couldn't handle my hands because I was moving too fast. I ain't stop punching though. I used all my strength and tossed her off me and stood up.

"Bitch, you ain't got shit else to say to me and keep

fucking playing with me I'mma really fuck yo ass up!" I yelled and she laughed.

"FUCK YOU KARTER! YOU JUST MAD BECAUSE YO NIGGA CANT KEEP HIS DICK IN HIS PANTS!" She shouted back, and I ran up on her and popped her two times.

Jania wasn't no match for me and she knew that. Shit, when we were in middle school I used to fight *her* battles. As soon as she fell backwards, I got on top of her and started raining blows wherever they could land.

"Man, what the fuck! Aye Little!" I heard Jamar bitch ass say and felt some arms grabbing me.

I wasn't done though. I grabbed Jania hair before Jamar carried me away and kicked her in the face.

"FUCK YOU BITCH! YOU BETTER TREAD LIGHTLY! I'M ON YO ASS! YOU KNOW HOW I GIVE IT UP!" I told her as Jamar let me go. Soon as I saw his face, I reached back and cracked his ass too. I grabbed my purse off the floor and stormed out of the house. Everybody was about to feel the wrath of Karter MOTHERFUCKING LYNN!

28

BRANDON

"Are you guys ready to see what y'all are having?" Doctor Jackie said as she squeezed some gel on Kris' stomach.

"Okay you guys.. I'm just guessing we are hoping for a boy... Since we have three girls. Am I right?" she asked, and we both looked at each other. It didn't bother me that much that Kris fucked around and got pregnant. I accepted the baby as my own. What bothered me was that Kris was keeping it a secret on who got her pregnant. I wasn't with that.

"I want a boy. I can't even lie." I smirked then Kris smiled. I kissed her forehead as the doctor waved her wand around Kris belly.

"Okay father. You got what you wanted. IT'S A BOY!" Doctor Jackie said and smiled big as me. The doc wiped the gel off and printed the ultrasounds.

"I will schedule your appointment two weeks out. I will see you later and congratulations." She said and walked out.

"So I get to pick the name." I said and she laughed as she gathered her stuff.

"Just get me some food, and we'll figure out what's next." Kris said and we got out of there. Our first stop was picking the girls up from Karter's house. When we pulled up to her house, the snow started to fall.

"We need to start Christmas shopping and getting into the spirit." Kris told me and I agreed.

Knock, knock, knock!

After a while, Karter came and opened the door for us. She was walking around sick as hell.

"What's wrong sis?" Kris asked as we followed her to the sitting room.

"This fucking baby is killing me!" Karter cried, and I laughed a little bit.

"Man, where the fuck is Jamar at man?" I asked and she smacked her lips.

"Bye Bran. Just go get y'all kids!" Karter said and I got up laughing.

I could hear Kris tell Karter she needed to get up and do something with herself. I shook my head and went upstairs to find the kids. Karter's house was big as hell so it took me a second to find the girls and they all were laying in Ashtyn's bed knocked out. I woke my oldest daughter Braylon up and she smiled looking at me. She hurried and grabbed her shoes and coat and quickly put it on. Brittyn did the same, and I grabbed baby girl and got her together so we could leave. When we got downstairs, I went straight to the door.

"Alright then Kar. Come on Kris." I called out and got the kids to the car so we could go eat.

∽

"THE KIDS ARE FINALLY SLEEP." Kris said climbing in the bed.

I guided her on top of me and she sat there for a minute. "Thank you Brandon." She spoke and I smiled.

"Thank you shorty." I told her and she blushed.

We have been through so much shit these past few years I was glad we were back together and finally in a happy place.

"I'm thinking about getting my tubes tied after this." Kris said and I nodded.

"I'm down for whatever you wanna do ma." I told her and she smiled. She kissed my lips and started to grind on me. "Take this off." I told her as I sat up and slipped my shirt off.

I kicked my pants off and laid back down as Kris climbed on top me again. Kris was sexy as hell, and this baby had her getting fat. I liked the extra meat on her body though. Kris started to play with my manhood as I kissed on her neck. I guided my dick in between her folds and she eased it inside.

"Shit Kris!" I snapped pushing my dick deep inside.

She started to bounce up and down, and I grabbed her waist. I had to start thinking about basketball, shit fishes. Something, because I didn't wanna nut prematurely. The way she was fucking me made me feel like a little bitch because she was taking the dick. I couldn't even fuck back!

"Damn shorty, slow down." I told her but she ain't listen.

The room was filled with splashing noises and her moaning. I was damn near whimpering because it was feeling so good. My stomach was hurting because I was sucking my stomach in so I wouldn't nut so fast. Damn, we been going at it for a good ten minutes, and I was already about to bury my seeds in her walls.

"FUCK KRIS." I moaned out biting my bottom lip.

She started to go slower so I flipped her over on her

stomach. I had to pull out quickly because I ain't wanna nut. I smacked her on the ass and she arched her back. Coating my dick with her juices, I went straight to work. Kris was showing out and matching my stroke. Every time I hit her spot, she squirmed.

"I'm about to come, don't stop Bran." She moaned out and I didn't.

I pulled the nut from out of both of us and collapsed on the side of her. Kris sat there for a second catching her breath, then she went to the bathroom and came back with a warm towel to wipe me off. She cuddled on my chest and we dozed off.

The next morning, I woke up to the smell of food. Kris wasn't next to me and usually when we slept in the girls would be in bed, but they weren't. I handled my hygiene first then went downstairs to see what everybody was doing. When I walked into the kitchen, I stopped in my tracks as I heard Kris talking on the phone.

"Look stop calling me. I told you my husband accepts my child. What do you mean you're gonna tell him?! Marcel, if you come to my husband with any of that bullshit he will murk yo stupid ass! WHY THE FUCK ARE YOU MAD BECAUSE MY HUSBAND ACCEPTS A BABY THAT YO ASS DONT EVEN FUCKING WANT! Look, I tried to be nice but now I'mma tell Jamar to fire yo ass. DON'T COME TO MY MOTHERFUCKING HOUSE NO MORE! And you better watch yo back." I heard Kris say and shook my head.

Marcel was who she was fucking while I was gone. That's why she ain't wanna tell me because she knew she was foul fucking with somebody in our fucking camp!

"Hey daddy." Braylon screamed as she saw me standing by the kitchen. I walked in and Kris was smiling awkwardly.

"Good morning." I said then kissed my kids' foreheads and then Kris' lips.

"Good morning babe. I was just about to wake you up." Kris said and I smiled.

"I gotta run somewhere then we can go get the stuff for the trip." I told Kris as we ate our breakfast. Little son's birthday was coming up so we were all going to Texas.

We were going for the weekend only because Christmas was coming up and nobody even started shopping. Plus, Karter and Jania was still into it with each other, so that would probably be just the right amount of time for them to get along.

"Alright, that's cool. We will be ready about time you come back love." Kris told me and we finished eating. After breakfast, I went to shower and dressed down in a black Nike sweatpants outfit. Grabbing my keys and making sure I was strapped I headed out to my destination.

Pulling up to the house, Marcel was getting into his car. I dialed Jamar and pulled off heading towards the warehouse.

"Hello?" Jamar answered on the last ring.

"What's up foo?" I greeted.

"Shit chilling out. What's up with you?" He asked and I sighed.

"Shit, out and about with it. You already know. Do me a solid one." I asked him and waited until he replied.

"What's good?" He asked me.

"Send Marcel a message saying meet you at the warehouse to pick you up." I told him, and Jamar didn't say nothing.

"What's going on?" Jamar asked and I contemplated on telling him.

"He disrespected in the worst way!" I told him straight up, and Jamar started typing away on his phone.

"It's done... Be safe bull." Jamar said, and we disconnected the call.

After a while, I pulled up behind the warehouse where we handle our business. Of course it was a few cars parked but Marcel wasn't there yet. I ducked off in the back of the parking lot and when Marcel pulled up I got out my car and jogged to where he parked at. He ain't even see me coming so as soon as I got close enough I swung and knocked his ass back to his car. Marcel stumbled back then shook the hits off.

"I knew you were going to be coming soon about that hoe." He taunted me, and I swung two more times dazing him. He came back with a punch, but I dodged it knocking him on his ass.

"You a snake ass nigga, and when I'm done burying yo bitch ass, I'mma make yo baby momma swallow my dick!" I smirked, and he came rushing me knocking me to the ground.

I was a beast with these hands so that little move didn't slow me down one bit. I wrestled my way on top and got to sending straight head shots. Every hit that connected to his head made him punch weaker and weaker. I was literally out here beating this nigga to death.

He started spitting up blood, but I ain't stop. He had me fucked up and, after I was done beating his ass to a pulp, I stood up. I aimed my gun to his head and he held his hand up but it was too late. I fired three shots aiming at his head killing him instantly. This snake ass nigga ain't deserve to be sent back to his family so I called the clean-up crew so they could get rid of him. Dreading heading home to deal with my snake ass wife.

29

CHARLES

"Who are you?" I asked some nigga sitting on the couch as I walked in my house.

Well, Mason and I were still living together as roommates of course. Matter of fact, we ended up finding a house big enough for the both of us and moved in it.

Mason and I were cool, and when he told me he wasn't straight, I did feel some type of way. Guaranteed I never asked him, but I poured out my whole life to this nigga. Told him secrets that I never spoke on and the fact this nigga just now telling me he was gay was a problem for me. So I kept my distance from him as much as possible.

"How are you? I'm Marcus, Mason friend." He stood up and tried to shake my hand. I rolled my eyes and went towards the stairs.

"What's up C?" Mason greeted as we passed each other on the steps.

I ignored him and walked to my bedroom. I was about to shower and go have lunch with Karter, Bria, and Kris.

Everything been good around these parts which I was

happy about. Tyree Jr's birthday went smooth and Karter and Jania didn't rip each other's heads off, but they still wasn't cool either. Christmas dinner wasn't no better, because it was at Karter house and Jania couldn't come. So her and Little did they own thing that was just horrible. Now here it is New Years, and it was going a little better. We all went to Club Head Huncho and partied. Of course Kris and Karter was miserable because they couldn't drink but we all had a ball.

Knock, knock, knock!

"Aye C, I am about to head out." Mason said coming into my room, but I didn't respond. I just kept my back to the door and him. "You good?" He asked and I sighed.

"I'm good. Have a good night." I snapped and the door shut.

"What's wrong with you?" Mason asked and I walked to my closet and started picking out me something to wear for tonight.

"I just don't understand why you're inviting strangers into our house? What, you fuck with him or something?" I asked clearly jealous.

It wasn't no secret that I had feelings for Mason. I'm not sure if it was because he saved me but I was feeling him heavily! I was feeling him way before I found out he was LGBT; that's probably why I was so mad that he told me after I confided in him so many times.

"That's where this attitude is coming from?" Mason asked and I rolled my eyes. I hated showing emotions now, and I hated when another person thought they had one up on me.

"Nah, you good." I said and he turned to walk away, but not before stopping and saying...

"You been walking around with an attitude with nobody

but me, so what's up?" He asked again, and I didn't say nothing.

"Go attend to your little date and have fun." I dismissed him, and he walked away this time slamming my door on his way out.

He annoyed me but he was right. I had an attitude with him. He was walking around like he didn't know I was feeling him. I'm not gone lie. I wasn't even in the mood to go out anymore. I sent a group chat message to the ladies cancelling and put my phone on do not disturb. After showering and slipping on my pajamas, I grabbed my smoke sack and went downstairs to the kitchen. I searched high and low for Mason's stash and found a new bottle of Patron. I filled my cup up with ice then went downstairs to where we turned the basement into a theater room.

The first movie I decided to watch was **Bad Boys**. I was in my own zone sipping my drink and smoking my blunt.

Finishing up my blunt, I thought back to my people. My real family, my father disowned me when I was only twelve for being attracted to men. My mother never tried to reach out to me, because she was so scared of my father. I had real siblings out here, but don't even know them or what they look like. It hurt me because I never had that fatherly love, and the love I always got came from Eva, her kids and their family. I had to do something nice for Momma E, because she took me in when I had nobody! I would have been lost or probably dead without them. That's why I fucked with Jamar so heavy because he was as loyal as they came.

After *Bad Boys* one went off, I went to *Bad Boys 2*. Halfway through the movie Mason came walking down the stairs. He was dressed in pajamas which means he must've been here for a minute.

"Wassup?" He asked and sat down next to me. He kicked

his feet up and got comfortable. At first, it was an awkward silence but I broke the tension.

"So how did your date go?" I asked Mason and he licked his lips. I turned my attention back to the T.V.

"Be honest with you? I couldn't even enjoy because I kept thinking about you." He said which made me roll my eyes.

I couldn't help but to think he was running game but something in me wanted to hear more. Even though I was extremely attracted to Mason, I didn't want to get involved and get my heart broken.

"Yeah, yeah tell me anything." I said and he smirked. He took a pre rolled blunt out the ashtray and fired it up.

"Dead ass. Why you think I'm home so early? We went to eat, we came back here, he got in his car and went home." Mason said, and I focused my attention on the T.V.

"So when was you gone tell me?" Mason asked and I looked at him. He wanted to keep talking, clouding my judgement when all I wanted was to just watch T.V. "Don't act like I'm getting on your nerves." Mason said as he smirked and I laughed. Mason was just so vibrant and had a good energy. That's probably what made me attracted to him.

"Yeah, I like you Mason. I see how you be with these other niggas so no I won't fall victim." I told him and he nodded.

"What if I told you, I wouldn't do you like how I do these other niggas." He said and I laughed out loud.

"I heard that before." I told him and he looked at me.

"You heard that before but not from me! I'm not those other niggas. Why you think I ran the streets day and night looking for them same motherfuckers who took you? Not revenge, because I always had feelings for you! I wasn't in this shit with y'all. I got in because they took you. Why you think I kept you so close? I haven't made a move on you because I know what you have been through. I know I wasn't ready for that type of commitment." Mason told me and I looked at him.

This nigga was laying it on me thick. I mean, I never knew these type of feelings was even present in him. He never gave no type of hints that he was interested in me.

"I hear you Mason. I'm…" He reached over the seat and kissed my lips. I pulled away and he sat back.

"I'm sorry. I didn't mean to…" Mason tried to say but I interrupted him.

"It's okay Mason." I said and he smirked and so did I.

"So you trying to fuck with ya boy or not?" Mason said and I playfully rolled my eyes.

∽

"No, it wasn't like that y'all! I was just not feeling well." I told Karter, Kris and Bria as they chewed me out for cancelling our date last night.

"Mhmm. Yeah okay. Just finish my shit!" Karter snapped, and I finished washing her hair. I was currently back doing hair but was doing it out of my house. Karter was going to school to do nails so once she gets her license we were gonna go half on our own building. I couldn't wait either!

"So you and Jamar still beefy?" I asked really concerned. I was confused for the most part because before I left Karter and Jamar never argued! So hearing Jamar getting somebody else pregnant, signing the divorce papers, leaving Kar and the kids was shocking to me. I feel for my girl, because I'm the one who sat up with her day and night while she expressed how much she loved Jamar for loving her and her son. Now it was like he was breaking her, and it wasn't my business unless she wanted me in it but I hated it!

"We not necessarily beefing but he not fucking with me and I'm not fucking with him. Neither are the kids." Karter shrugged and I nodded.

"Well..." Bria caught us off guard jumping up running to the bathroom.

"Oowee! If one pregnant, y'all all pregnant! Let me call this bitch Jania and see if she knocked up." I joked and we laughed. I was dead ass for real though! These kids in the family was gone be close as hell because they all got somebody in their age range. I'm pretty sure Bria ass knocked up too. She was sitting over there looking pleasantly plump.

"So when you gone have the wedding?" Karter asked Kris and she sighed.

Kris been walking around looking like a sad puppy for the past week or so, and I'm just trying to figure out who killed her dog.

"Okay, I wasn't gone speak on it but you killing the mood. What's been wrong with you?" I asked blow drying Karter's hair so I could braid it up. Meanwhile, Bria came back in looking at us salty.

"Well congratulations." I told her and she flipped me off.

"Not in the mood." She told me as she sat down popping a peppermint in her mouth.

"Back to you miss thang. What's been wrong with you?" I asked Kris again and she sighed.

"Okay you guys, I think Bran found out I was messing with Marcel then killed him." She whispered the last part like she ain't just drop a big bomb on us that she was fucking Jamar driver, Marcel.

"MARCEL!?" I yelled dragging out the L.

She snapped her neck at me trying to keep me quiet like

it was somebody else in this big ass house. Mason went out earlier and hasn't been back and right now I haven't told anybody about us two so I was hoping he ain't come back until they were gone.

"Okay y'all, yes, I was fucking with Marcel. Brandon had to have found out because now he's missing and his wife been calling asking was he with me because she knew this whole time or whatever. I'm just sick of it." Kris said.

"Then I don't wanna ask him about it because what if he don't know and be like why you looking for Marcel and it be bullshit." She went on and I looked at her. I could tell she was worried about the situation but she had to move on and come clean.

"Just next time he asks about your baby's father come clean and say it's Marcel's. If he be nonchalant then he knows and he did it. If he be mad and do the most he don't know and you gotta figure out who killed your other baby dad!" Bria said which I agreed.

"Yeah, I agree with sis." I said as I started to braid her hair. Mason came jogging down the stairs looking sexy as ever. No we weren't together but we had an understanding and was working on getting ourselves together for each other.

"What's up y'all. What's up sis?" He greeted kissing everyone on the cheek. When he got to me he didn't hesitate to peck me on the lips leaving everybody mouth open.

When he walked away, the questions started coming in.

"What the fuck? Mason is gay?" Kris dumb ass asked and I laughed. Karter did too, because she knew.

"When did y'all become this? I mean, what's going on?" Kris asked feeling salty and I laughed..

"I mean, we just chilling; nothing major." I said and left the conversation at that.

"C?" Mason came to the steps and the girls shut they mouth and I laughed.

"Yes?" I yelled back.

"We going out tonight so don't make any plans." He told me.

"Yes daddy." Karter joked and we laughed.

"Alright!" I smiled feeling the butterflies in my stomach. I could get used to this attention again.

30

MACE

"What's wrong with you? You don't feel good?" I asked Bria as she laid in the bed. She has been like this ever since she got her hair done yesterday.

"I'm pregnant Mace." She said like it was the end of the world.

"Okay, you don't wanna keep it?" I asked. I was down with whatever my wife wanted. If she wasn't ready for another kid then we could do what she wanted to do. I mean, I wanted another kid but I can wait. It ain't no pressure.

"What you mean do I wanna keep it?" She asked clearly insulted.

"You just didn't seem too happy to announce the news to me." I told her.

"I'm with whatever you with. Of course, I would love for you to have another one of my babies." I continued and she smirked.

"I didn't know how you would act. Our baby girl is only about to be two." Bria spoke and I nodded.

"You not leaving me, and I'm not leaving you. So it doesn't matter." I told her and kissed her lips.

"Now since we got this under control, please get up and do something with ya self. I'm tired of seeing this bonnet." I told her and she laughed.

"Babe, did you know Charles and Mason goes together?" She asked me and I nodded.

"Yeah, Mason tell me everything." I told her and she gasped.

"And you didn't tell me? WOW!" She said dragging the W at the end of wow. I laughed.

"Yeah babe. I been knowing he had feelings for C since before he found C. Shit, I'm surprised you ain't peep. Why do you think he was going so hard to find out who did it? We just ain't know C was still alive." I told her and she got up. Bria went to the bathroom, and I went to my son Montana's room. He was playing the game with his headset on.

"What's up dad!" Montana said as he stood in the middle of the floor with his controller in the hand. "Come this way cuz. Come on, before he kill you!" he yelled and got hype. "Ask aunty can you and Karson come over?" he spoke into the headset and looked back at me.

"Pops, can cousins come over?" He asked and I nodded.

"Come on, let's go get them." I told him and he got hype. I went back to the room and Bria was walking out of the bathroom with her towel wrapped around her.

"Let's go get the boys from Karter's and go eat somewhere." I told her and she agreed. I sat on the edge of the bed and waited until she got dressed. She gathered our daughter Brielle out her Pack and Play then we left.

. . .

PULLING UP TO KARTER'S, Jamar was pulling up also. He knocked on the door as we got out.

"What up bro?" Jamar greeted and hugged Bria.

Karter came to the door then opened it.

"KJ just told me y'all was coming. I just got they clothes on." She said out of breath. Karter always been pretty while she was pregnant, but this time she looked tired.

"You okay sis?" I asked as I followed her up the stairs to the girls' room.

"Yes, just sleepy. This little baby is giving me hell!" She said, and I kissed her forehead

"I hope you feel better. I'll keep the boys for the weekend." I told her.

"Alright, that's fine! Thank you bro. Jamar about to take the girls. You got yo key. Can you lock up?" She said and weakly smiled. I couldn't put my finger on it, but something was different about Karter. I think she was really sick. She walked to her room, and I gathered all the kids downstairs.

"Let me holla at you bro before you leave." I told Jamar. After we got the kids into each car, Jamar stood outside of my car waiting on me.

"What's up with sis? She don't look good?" I asked and he sighed.

"I thought it was just normal pregnancy symptoms, but the more I see her, the more I see she doesn't look like she is getting better. She don't wanna talk to me because she still mad about the abortion shit." Jamar told me, and I sighed then ran my hand down my face.

"Have you been going to the appointments?" I asked him.

"She hasn't been. She ain't schedule one yet." Jamar said, and I looked at him like he was dumb.

"Bro, you need to fix that! Sis doing bad right now, and I

ain't never saw her this fucked up. If you ain't gone do right then leave her alone, but you got her out here looking bad." I told him straight up and he nodded. "Take her to an appointment and see what's up." I dabbed him up and walked away. Our first stop was Dave and Busters since we wanted to eat and have fun.

31

LITTLE

"What's up big bro?" Santana, Jamar's cousin, said as we walked into the meeting. Jamar and I have been talking about getting out of the game for a while now. So I called Santana and his brother Montana to see how they would like to expand. They did their own thing with the drugs and shit but we did bigger things. I know if they wanted to accept our offer, they definitely could handle it. The little nigga San reminded me of Jamar back when Jamar was his age, and Montana was more like me. Both these little niggas was crucial though.

"What it do family?" I asked them as we sat down.

I didn't include Charles and Brandon in this meeting, because they had given up the drug game a long time ago. Bran just started investing into more clubs and now he trying to do restaurants. Jamar was supposed to come, but he had to go take sis to the doctor. I still fucked with Kar even though she wasn't fucking with Jania. Shit, they were best friends at the end of the day. I'm not sure how they rocked before I met Jania, so I wasn't getting in the middle of that.

"Where big cuz at?" Santana asked me.

"He had to take care of wifey." I told him and he nodded.

I explained to San and Montana on why we're getting out of the game. It was time for us to pass the torch down. I was gonna take them under my wing and school them on how we ran it, and if they liked it they could take over and just pay Jamar and I a percentage. They gladly accepted the offer and wanted to get to work ASAP. That's what I'm talking about when I say they remind me of me and Jamar; the hustle in them is what I love.

To celebrate our deal, we went out to the club. I couldn't wait until Jamar and I opened our strip club because it wasn't no good booty clubs in the city. We were about to take over the club scene. We already had a few Head Honchos that was around the country, so I was just waiting to get my hands out the drug game to dive in head first into the legal world.

"I'm glad y'all was interested in this. Jamar and I hands are tied. We getting older, and it's our time to leave this game alone." I told them and they both nodded paying attention to what I was saying. I have been in the game for a long time. By the grace of God, I'm leaving voluntary. I was just glad the empire was staying in the family, and we were passing it down to some people we trusted.

∽

"I THINK we should get T-2 that one." Jania said pointing to a convertible Power Wheel. It was a day before Christmas Eve, and we were last minute shopping.

"Alright, that's cool. We got everything on they list." I told her and she nodded.

I couldn't wait until it was over. We all were meeting at

Momma E house tomorrow for the family Secret Santa, but I was ready for Christmas day. I had so much in store for my family I couldn't wait to see their faces.

"I'm going to try and reach out to Kar one more time." Jania said and I nodded. I wish they could just get it together. I had to get in Jamar ass for putting my girl in the middle of his shit. If he was gone fuck off he should've did it with outside females.

"Just let her be. When she is ready to talk, she will reach out to you." I told her and she nodded.

"Well, I think I'm ready to get back in school. Do these classes for this day care. " Jania said and I smiled.

"I'm proud of you shorty. I'm with whatever you wanna do." I responded as we paid for the toys.

After we finished shopping, we went home. It took me a few trips to hide the toys in the stash. I went into the kitchen where the kids was sitting at the table eating.

"Hey dad. I need to talk to you?" Ty'aira said and stood up.

"Hey baby girl?" Jania said and Ty'aira ignored her which was odd. Ty'aira loved Jania!

"What's up princess?" I asked and picked her up. She hesitated for a second, and I could tell something was weighing on her shoulder.

"Dad, please don't lie. I heard nana talk and she says mommy hurt my other mommy." Ty'aira said and my heart dropped to my stomach. "Dad, I'm sorry. I shouldn't have said anything." She said and tried to wiggle out my arms, but I couldn't let her go. I held her tightly and sighed.

Jania wasn't standing too far from us, but she had her hand over her mouth with tears in her eyes. I knew she wanted to come comfort Ty'aira, but she knew it wasn't a good idea. I sat Ty'aira down on the counter and stood in front of her.

"Remember when I said bad people was trying to hurt daddy? Well, your other mommy was one of those bad people. Jania was only protecting us." I told her and she nodded.

"I'm not mad. Nana said I should be happy because I have my other mommy to love me. I'm just sad because I don't want mommy to leave again." Ty'aira said and I nodded.

"SHE WON'T! I promise that we will never leave you. Neither me or mommy." I told her and she hugged me. Jania sat down next to me and Ty'aira hugged her.

"I love you Ty Ty. Don't ever think otherwise." Jania told her and they hugged again. "Now go eat." Jania told her and slapped her butt. Jania went back to the table with the kids while she fixed our plates and heated them up.

Ring, Ring, Ring!

"Hello?" I answered my phone for Jamar.

"What it do bro? What are you on?" Jamar asked me.

"Shit, just walked in the door. I called you this morning. How sis feeling?" I asked as Jania sat the plate down in front of me.

"She doing good. They gave her some medicine because she had a UTI and some other shit. She should be feeling better. How was the meeting?" He asked me all in one breath.

"It went good. We about to start training them our way. They ready though." I told him. I was just ready to get out and start doing my own thang.

"Was they cool with the percentage?" He asked and I smirked.

"Yeah, they was player as fuck. They are ready to apply

pressure. I can't wait to see these little niggas in action!" I said and we both laughed.

"I knew them niggas was perfect for the job." Jamar said and I agreed. After we talked about what we had planned, Jamar and I disconnected the call.

After eating, we headed to the sitting room so we could chill out and watch a movie.

32

KRIS

"Babe, just put the sweater on." I told Brandon as he walked around with an attitude.

This nigga been in his feelings since I finally told him about me and Marcel which I'm confused about because he already killed the nigga! Hell, I should be the one walking 'round this bitch with an attitude.

"I'm not wearing that. I'm ready!" Brandon snapped and I looked at him.

"What's wrong with you?" I snapped and he sighed.

"I'm not wearing a sweater." Brandon said again which made me roll my eyes.

"Okay, that's cool, but I said what's wrong with you?" I asked again.

"Look, I don't think this is gonna work. I can't fuck with you like that." Brandon said which pissed me off.

"What? Who is it? Cause you been moving real funny lately!" I snapped and he laughed.

"I found somebody else and I'm just about to go spend time with her for Christmas. I'll be back tomorrow to see my kids open they toys." Brandon said, and I laughed to hide the way I was really feeling. I can't even lie. I believe everything he said. I knew Brandon well and I know when he moving foul. He been staying out late, going out the room to talk on the phone, and I don't even wanna think about him being on drugs again but damn! Shit ain't been peaches since he found out about Marcel but he said he forgive me and that we're moving on but this ain't moving on.

"So you're gonna go over there and tell our kids why their father isn't coming! You're gonna tell your kids that, not me!" I yelled getting into his face. He held his hands up blocking me from hitting him. My big belly was stopping me from swinging.

"I'M GOING! TAKE ME THERE!" I yelled feeling the tears form in my eyes.

"Girl, you trippin. I'm not taking you over there." Brandon said so nonchalantly which pissed me off even more.

"YOU TAKING ME! I'M GOING!" I yelled as the tears came down. "Fuck you Brandon." I snapped as I grabbed my coat and purse. He went to the closet and grabbed a duffle bag I guess he already packed and I laughed.

"You got me so fucked up Brandon." I stated calmly as he followed me down the stairs. I went to the passenger side of his truck and got in. He came out of the house and got in the driver's seat and drove off.

"Why even ask me to marry you and you knew you don't wanna be with me?" I asked as more tears fell. I knew it was the baby that had me crying because if it was any other time I would have been laid hands on Brandon.

"Don't ask questions that you know you don't want to know the answers to!" Brandon said and turned the radio up. Little did he know when we get to this house, him and whatever bitch he wanted to creep with was dead!

. . .

When we pulled up to the bitch house, the tears dried instantly. I mean, shorty was living in a nice ass brick house. The driveway had a round-about with a water fountain in the middle.

"Damn." I mumbled. Her house put ours to shame for real. I cringed at the thought of Brandon buying this nice ass house for her. It was a four car garage connected to the house and a black G-Wagon was parked with a red ribbon in front.

"Brandon, I swear to God I'm about to kill you and this bitch! Let me out this car!" I cried as he pulled the door opened as the car came to a complete stop. I didn't even wait until he got out. I ran to the front door and pounded on the door. I wasn't even gonna attempt to kick it down. The door itself looked like it weighed more than me.

"Open this door bitch!" I yelled pounding. Brandon grabbed my arm and swung me around.

"Chill the fuck out! You know how much this fucking door cost me!" He yelled, and all sense went out the window as he pulled out a set of keys to open the door.

"Bitch, you got me messed up!" I yelled and started hitting him in the back as he pushed the door open. The smell of new house hit me and the house was so beautiful and empty.

"Merry Christmas wifey." He smirked and held the keys up.

"BRANDON!" I yelled looking around. He had this big, goofy smile on his face, and I just stood there. I just looked around trying to take in the fact that he wasn't fucking around on me. He actually bought me a house and car for Christmas.

"Take a picture you guys!" Janet said as Brandon, the kids, and I walked into her house.

She had the whole house decorated with Christmas stuff and colors. I see she was one of the few in the Christmas spirit but after the gifts Bran gave me I was happy. He was literally a different person after the rehab and I loved him for it. We were getting married again on Valentine's day, and he bought me my own house! I couldn't wait to have my son and be a completed family.

"Yes sis! Y'all look so cute!" Karter said taking our picture also. Karter was finally back glowing and getting big. I think she's having another boy because every time she gets pregnant with a boy her hips and butt spread wide as hell.

"Thanks sis! You look like you feeling better." I told her and she smiled widely.

"I am feeling better." She told me as we went to the living room where the rest of the family was occupied. The kids went to go play, while we sat around and waited for the rest of the family to get here.

Charles wasn't lying when he said if one was pregnant then we all were. Bria was mad she couldn't smoke with the guys because Mace done got her pregnant, Karter couldn't drink but Jamar did let her have some wine. I, on the other hand, was chilling. I just couldn't wait to get home so I could have some alone time with Brandon. I was so in love and happy with him. I needed to do something special for him to show him how much I love and appreciate him.

33

JANIA

"Hey Karter, can I talk to you for a minute?" I asked Karter as she talked to Eva and Janet. She smiled and so did I. Karter looked so much happier and vibrant since the last time I saw her. She's pregnant so I know she won't try to fight me this time. I was just ready to put the beef shit behind us so we could be back cool again. I missed my friend.

"What's up Jania?" She asked me as I pulled her to the kitchen for some privacy.

"You look gorge!" I told her and she smiled.

"Thank you!" She responded and I nodded,

"I apologize for not telling you about Jamar and Lilly. She had just told me right before you came and I didn't have enough time to tell you. I mean, we talked since then but I just feel like the love isn't there anymore. I know we won't ever be back like we used to be but I'm sorry Karter. I have been going through my own shit, fucked up from what them people did to me. I was being a fake ass friend to you and I shouldn't have because you been here for me this whole time!" I told her and she nodded taking in everything I said to her.

"I just want us to get passed it all. Even if we don't become real good friends like we were. I just want us to be talking because I miss you." I told her truthfully and she smiled. Which made me smile.

"I'm sorry but I could never look at you like my friend again. You said some hurtful shit and I forgive you but I won't give you another chance to betray me. No love lost or beef. We cool." Karter said and hugged me. "I got my nephews and niece some stuff also in my truck. Remind me to get it out before we all leave!" Karter told me and we went back to the sitting room where everybody was playing games and having a good time.

After we ate and played a few games, everyone exchanged gifts. I was just happy everything went off without drama. Plus, I know Eva was going through some stuff with Tiera being gone but I was happy she was in a good mood. I had a long talk with her also, and I'm glad she didn't hold me accountable on how shit went with Tiera. I must say this was one of the best Christmas's that I have had in a long time.

Waking up the next morning on Christmas day, the kids came into our room jumping on the bed. The smell of food filled the room quickly and my stomach growled. I was happy Little talked me into getting Eva housemaid Linda to come over and help me with things. I know she was downstairs throwing down in the kitchen.

"It's Christmas! Wake up mommy! Wake up daddy!" Tyaira screamed as I turned over.

"Good morning." I yawned and went to the bathroom to handle my hygiene. I walked back to my bedroom, and Little was up getting Jayda out her crib while the kids jumped around trying to get us to hurry up so they could open their gifts.

"Good morning shorty." Little said then kissed my lips with his morning breath.

"Okay babes. You go handle that breath while we wait downstairs for you." I told him and reached for my baby girl.

She was wide awake smiling and drooling over her daddy. Jayda was literally my twin though. She had my complexion and my face. Only thing she had was Little's good ass hair. I kissed her little fingers and she laughed. It took a long while for me to get to this place, and I was just happy I could hold my baby girl without feeling any negative thoughts. Jayda was the most perfect baby ever! She didn't cry at all; all she did was laugh and smile. The name fit her perfectly because she was very pretty.

After Little handed me Jayda, the kids followed me downstairs. I went to the kitchen first and grabbed a bottle from the fridge and put it in the warmer. I still breastfeed but I hardly give her the nipple, only the bottles.

"Good morning." I told Linda as she walked in the kitchen. Linda reminded me of an older grandmother. She was so sweet and real. She gave me the best advice and was the mother figure that I needed.

"Good morning." She smiled and winked at me.

We went to the family room, and I sat down on the floor in front of the tree while I finished feeding Jayda. Little came down the stairs with a few boxes and sat them in front of me.

"Alright, let's start?" Little said and the kids jumped up and down. Ty went to the biggest boxes he saw and Tyaira read the names off.

Me and Little cleaned the house and sent the kids off to play with their toys so that we could do our gift exchange.

"You go first." Little said and I smirked. I couldn't wait so I opened the first box and it was the smallest one with a charm bracelet from Tiffany's. I squealed because it was already filled with charms and I held my wrist up so he could help me put it on.

"Thank you baby!" I smiled and kissed him. I couldn't even stop smiling and laughing opening the other gifts. Even though I get nice stuff all year around. I was happy right now. The second box was a Chanel purse with the matching boots, which is what I had in my cart online. I got excited opening up the boxes because it was like Little was in my head. He literally got me everything that I wanted without even asking him for it.

"You deserve it all baby." Little said then kissed my lips. I stood up and went to the Christmas tree and grabbed the smallest box.

"Because I feel like you have been taking care of everybody other than yourself I got you something that I think you would love." I told him and he opened the box. He held up the key fob with a smile on his face. I followed him to the door and a 2019 blue Challenger Hellcat with tents and customized rims was parked in our driveway. I spent a pretty penny on it but it was worth it. I was just happy we all had a great Christmas.

KARTER AND JAMAR

The whole family was sitting around the house waiting for me to push the baby out. We have a seafood broil prepared for everyone. I been sitting in this pool forever waiting to push this little baby out. It was indeed my last baby so I was prepared to go big or go home. That's why I was doing a home water birth and had the whole family here to support me. I had a chef here because once I got this baby out and fed I was gone pump and have me a drink and enjoy me some good ass soul food. I couldn't wait. I was even more eager to push this damn baby out!

We had a photographer who was going to make this a movie that we could have forever and ever to watch. I didn't have any meds and these contractions was kicking my ass but I was handling them well. My midwife never left my side. She was at my beck and call whenever I needed her to be. Our main mission was to have this baby!

"Miranda, I think it's time." I told her. It was like the whole house got quiet all at once and everyone's attention was on me.

"You sure bae?" Jamar asked.

"Yes, are you getting in the water with me?" I asked as a contraction hit. It's been seven hours of nonstop contractions, and I have been taking this shit like a straight gangster. My family hasn't been any extra stress, and I even put my pride to the side and let Jania be a part of this too. At the end of the day, she is my best friend.

"Get my bestie some lip gloss; she can't be on camera with these dry ass lips." Jania said to no one in particular. Little brought over her purse and she did me a quick face beat and made sure my lips was popping. Charles finished me off with putting my hair up in a pretty, messy bun.

"Now let's have this baby suh." Charles said and we high-fived.

Everybody around the room said how proud they was of me and when it got to Jamar he got choked up. He removed his clothes down to his Ethika draws. A contraction hit which made me close my eyes and when I reopened them to see why my kids' father wasn't in this damn water with me I was surprised as hell.

"Karter, you mean the world to me. I've made some mistakes and realize that I got to fix them muthafuckas. I be so sick without you, trying to find a feeling that you give me, and never have I ever. Long story short, I love you and all my shorties so what I'm trying to say is will you marry me? Again?" Jamar said. By this time the tears were coming full throttle out of my eyes as another contraction hit, and I had to catch my breath before I answered. Once the contraction passed I finally spoke.

"Of course I will marry you baby." I told him and he had a big Kool-Aid smile on his face.

"Now let's focus on this baby." Jamar said sliding the ring on my finger and kissed me passionately. He slid inside of the pool of water with me, and my baby must've just known because I got the urge to push.

"Dad, it might be easier if she gets up on her knees and you stay behind her and catch baby as it slides out ok?" Miranda said. The doctor pulled me forward, and I was on all fours. I felt like my baby was right at the opening bout to come out.

"I have to push. I feel the baby coming out." I told Miranda.

"Your next contraction, push Kar." Jamar told me.

As it came, I pushed hard as I could until it passed.

"You doing good, Karter; the baby head is poking out. One more push and baby will be here." Miranda said to me.

I looked up and looked around, and everybody looked more nervous than me. I looked back at Jamar and this nigga was sweating like he was doing the pushing. I felt another contraction coming on, and I pushed hard as hell cause at this point I was becoming exhausted. I screamed out as I pushed and felt so relieved. Jania and Kris was both crying and screaming out of excitement. I turned around to join Jamar with holding our precious little girl. We never told anyone the gender so it could be a surprise but I knew all along.

"What we naming her bae?" Jamar asked.

"Phor'Ever My'luv Jackson. I know it's breaking the J and K's but this our last baby; it's only right she gets this." I told her.

"That's perfect." Eva and Jamar said at the same time and I smiled. I laid my head on Jamar's chest next to where the baby was laying and just stared at her. This baby was a perfect mixture of me and Jamar. I was in love with her already.

"Hey Chef, can you get the soul food started? I'm ready

to eat!" I yelled to the chef and he walked away to go get the job done.

∼

"She's beautiful as hell, Jamar. I can't stop staring at her." My mom told me.

It's been three months since she was born, and my mom was taking her so that I could continue getting ready for the wedding. It felt different this time around though. After watching Phor'Ever be born, who I gave the nickname Ever, I found a new respect for Karter. I always watch her give birth but not in that state. It just opened my eyes, and I was sitting here praying and thanking God that she's giving me another chance. I spent a mil to make sure my baby felt like a princess today, and I can't wait to see how beautiful she looks when she's walking down the aisle.

Our colors were white, pink and lavender, colors picked by the wife of course. It all came together so tight though. My wife was definitely hard at what she did here, and I'm gonna put a business proposition in her ear. I know her heart was with esthetics and I had a surprise for her and Charles after the wedding as well. I had ten minutes till the wedding begin so I put on my blazer and went to get in stance. Standing there, *All My Life by K-Ci and JoJo* started to play and she appeared. She was so beautiful, man, my dick got hard and tears stung my eyes. How the fuck can one person have this effect on you? That's Karter muthafuckin Jackson for you though. That's why I was honored to be getting a second time to make her Mrs. Taylor!

We exchanged vows and it wasn't a dry eye in the room which I didn't know why. Everybody knows wassup with us and how we feel about each other. I had an announcement to make before we changed though so Little came forward with two blindfolds after we jumped the broom.

"Bae, before we ride off into the sunset and change for the after party I got something I wanna show you but you gotta put this blindfold on." I told her.

"Well, who's the second one for?" I didn't answer her until I had hers tied up.

"C, my nigga, come here." I told him as he looked shocked as hell walking towards me.

"I'mma lead you, Kar, and you gone lead me. Everybody else, y'all just follow." We had over two hundred people here with us so it took us a minute to walk through. There were a few ohh and awws during the walk which irritated me because they see my wife blindfolded and knowing her hard-headed ass she'll pull it right off.

"Man, it's so many of us present, and I just wanna thank y'all again for coming out for this special day. I see my main folks present so I'mma go ahead and start. They been working their ass off tryna get this together. I just wanted to help them because what they do for each of us standing here in this room doesn't go unnoticed. Remove the blindfolds kiddos." I told them.

They both eagerly snatched the blindfolds off, and Karter dramatic ass started jumping up and down screaming. C wiped a lone tear that dropped, and we shook up and he hugged me.

"Now baby, I know yo heart is with esthetics and that's why I chose this building for the wedding. When you told me you wanted to do the wedding yourself and spent all my money I'm like what could she possibly be doing with this much money but as y'all see she did her shit. This entire building is you and Charles's so maybe y'all can get into event planning next. I don't give a damn; it's up to y'all.

Cheers to the new business owners!" I yelled and everybody started to applaud and cheer them on. It was time to party now, and I was more than ready to end the night with my wife. **Mace and Bria**

"I'm thinking about doing a water birth as well. But not with the whole damn family present shit." I told Mace as we laid in bed eating pizza and wings. I got up and wobbled to the bathroom because these damn babies was sitting dead on my bladder.

"But you having twins. Wouldn't it be risks?" He asked me.

"Yeah, but my nurse would still come out to the house to deliver me. And she'll have her backup team ready in case something does go wrong. Money talks hubby." I told him washing my hands and rejoining him in the bed.

"Whatever you want my love; the world is yours." He told me. We have been so happy lately. We hardly ever worked and could spend more time with our family and friends. I was loving it. Maybe we should've combined our families a long time ago.

∼

I COULDN'T WAIT for Bria to have these babies so I could pop some more into her. I love my wife, and I would give her ten babies if she lets me. I enjoy the father and husband role, and I wouldn't trade it for nothing in this world. Bria's idea worked out for the better. We been straight ever since we brought together her father and the BGF. I been making more money than before and hardly ever working.

"Aye wife, I love you." I told Bria.

"I love you more hubby." she told me and embraced for a kiss.

"I been liking this hardly ever working life and being able to be at home more. I think we should expand our business and bring more people on." I told her.

"I'm down with whatever you with. I can train them the same way you trained me and we'd be unstoppable." She told me with a smirk. I trained one bad ass broad. No disrespect to my wife but she could kill you in a split second with no remorse. Yeah, I did that for sure. Life was just coming together perfectly for us and as long as my family is happy, I'm happy.

Mason and Charles

"How did Jamar know exactly what I wanted?" I asked suspiciously.

"I don't know babe, probably Karter." Mason answered.

"I've never even mentioned it to nobody." I told him more clear so that he will get the hint. An awkward silence passed before he spoke up.

"Okay babe, me and Jock both invested into your and Karter's dreams. All the late night talks about what you wanted was put into play. I love you. I just want the best for you." He told me and I almost cried. No man has ever put that much thought and time into me to where they doing shit like this. I just might love it here after all.

~

CHARLES WAS in his beauty room making Karter a wig, and I just felt like this was the perfect time to ask before I chickened out for the hundredth time. His back was facing me which was perfect. I got down on one knee. I just watched him as he moved around the mannequin head and was kinda amazed. He was a beast in the hair business. Everybody wanted CiCi to touch their head as they called him up at his shop. I was so caught up in watching him I didn't even know that he was alert of me being in the room.

"Babe..." he said.

"Charles, I've always had a thing for you and no one knew but my brother. That's why when you came up missing I went so hard to find out who did it and how to get you back. When I thought you were dead, I knew I was gone get payback for taking my loved one before I could confess my love. I just want to know will you marry me?" I asked him.

"You know I will. Yes!" He said hurriedly.

"Now we ain't bout to have no big ass wedding like Kar did. I'm simple." He told me.

"Maybe sis can do the wedding for us." I suggested.

"I'd love that. She knows me best." He agreed.

"I love you so much." I told him.

"I love you too. Thank you. For everything." He told me, and we kissed and went on to plan our honeymoon and wedding and also our adoption that we've been putting a lot of our time into lately.

Little and Jania

I was so happy to be back on good terms with Karter. We ain't how we was growing up but it'll do. The big countdown is real for our wedding coming up in less than three months, and I absolutely could not wait. I was so proud of us because like everyone else we deserve to be happy. After everything we've gone through together it was only right Little put a ring on it. I'm so in love with the family I've created. Nothing else in this world matters to me but them.

Everyone around us has been opening businesses, and I've heard her mention a daycare a few times in the past. I got all the paperwork together that was needed for *Nini's Tiny Tots* daycare to open. I started having renovations done as soon as I got the keys to the building in my hand. I was getting ready to have her meet with me for lunch so that I could take her over and surprise her ass with it. She went through a lot for dealing with me so I owe lil mama the world. She been thuggin with the kidnapping, baby momma drama, beef with Karter, even the shit she went through with her ex-nigga. Baby girl just deserve some happiness. After lunch at Ruth Chris, she followed me to the building.

"What the fuck are you about to do? Kill me or something. Why are we at an abandoned building?" Jania asked me. I had to laugh cause she say the wildest shit.

"Nah man surprise, this is yours. Pull them curtains down." I told her chuckling at her goofy ass.

"Nini's Tiny Tots," she said more so to herself. "Is this my... my daycare?" She asked me.

"Yeah bae." I told her confidently.

"I don't know if I'm pregnant again or what but I've been real emotional lately. I can't even deal with this right now." She told me walking away wiping her tears.

"Come here baby. After everything you been through you really deserve it. Come on, let's go home and talk about prices and colors of each room. That type of shit. We can come back and see it later." I told her as she grabbed my hand. Cheers to my baby's new beginnings!

Brandon and Kris

. . .

AFTER KRIS HAD our son I was set. Of course over time I was going to want to produce my own son. Don't get me wrong, blood couldn't make me and Brandon Jr any stronger. I just want my blood running through my son's veins. Ain't nothing wrong with that right? Ever since he got here it's been perfect for us. We were in a new home with a new baby and it felt like a new start.

∼

EVER SINCE BRANDON took Marlo he had been this new person. I was so grateful. I felt like part of the reason why Brandon loved BJ so much is because he took his biological father, but I ain't ever speak of it. The girls were loving their new baby brother, and this little boy was more spoiled than any of the girls ever was. I'm glad everything worked out for the better, and I'm actually content with life. Life is amazing; it is what it should be. Everyone who was a part of the BGF got their fairytale ending. Peace!

SUBSCRIBE

Text Shan to 22828 to stay up to date with new releases, sneak peeks, contest, and more....

SUBMISSIONS

To submit your manuscript to Shan Presents, please send
the first three chapters and synopsis
to submissions@shanpresents.com

CPSIA information can be obtained
at www.ICGtesting.com
Printed in the USA
LVHW091738120220
646719LV00003B/407